But he couldn't have everything he wanted in less than a week.

An awesome job and a girlfriend to boot. Could he?

"You look like something's on your mind."

"I. . .uh, I'm happy to have a friend. When you're new in town, a friend is awesome."

"It's important. Friends make things better. And so can ice cream when you've had a tough day. I get a cone whenever I've had a tough day." She paused as if lost in her own thoughts.

"Has today been a tough day?"

"No, it's been pretty good, actually."

Dan was liking this more and more. He'd give it a few more days, tops. Jo was sure to be in his relationship status on Facebook. He hoped.

LAURALEE BLISS, a former nurse, is a prolific writer of inspirational fiction as well as a home educator. She resides with her family near Charlottesville, Virginia, in the foothills of the Blue Ridge Mountains—a place of inspiration for many of her contemporary and historical novels. Lauralee Bliss writes inspirational fiction to provide readers with entertaining stories intertwined with Christian principles to assist them in their day-to-day walk with the Lord. Aside from writing, she enjoys gardening, cross-stitching, reading, roaming yard sales, and traveling. Lauralee invites you to visit her Web site at http://www.lauraleebliss.com.

Books by Lauralee Bliss

HEARTSONG PRESENTS
HP249—Mountaintop
HP333—Behind the Mask
HP457—A Rose among Thorns
HP538—A Storybook Finish
HP569—Ageless Love
HP622—Time Will Tell
HP681—The Wish
HP695—Into the Deep
HP755—Journey to Love
HP783—Seneca Shadows

Love's Winding Path

Lauralee Bliss

Heartsong Presents

For all those with prodigal sons and daughters. . .
there is hope!

A note from the Author:
I love to hear from my readers! You may correspond with me by writing:

Lauralee Bliss
Author Relations
PO Box 721
Uhrichsville, OH 44683

ISBN 978-1-60260-707-1

LOVE'S WINDING PATH

Our mission is to publish and distribute inspirational products offering exceptional value and biblical encouragement to the masses.

PRINTED IN THE U.S.A.

one

"When are you planning to help out around here?"

Dan glanced out the corner of his eye at his older brother, Rob, clad in mud-streaked jeans and boasting smears of dirt on each cheekbone. Dan smirked and returned to his magazine on river rafting. What a spectacle Rob was, standing there like Farmer John from the back hills. He ought to be playing a mouth harp and doing the jig to complete the picture.

"I'm taking a break," Dan informed him, flipping a page in the magazine.

"You've been on a break for the last few years around here," Rob grumbled. "When are you gonna snap out of it? Pop knows how much you sit around here doing nothing."

"Aren't you a little old at twenty-seven to be ratting?" Dan snapped, scanning an article on the best places to raft along the Colorado River. He ignored Rob's complaining and returned to important business at hand. Like seeking another career. . .and another life. How he would love to be one of those river guides in the rafts, though he knew nothing of it, save the one trip he took a few years back in West Virginia. Even then he remembered the thrill of the trip in foaming white water, manning his paddle with vigor while trying to keep himself in the boat. And out in Utah, surrounded by raw, red cliffs glistening in the hot sun, the weather was sweltering but different from steamy Virginia with the humidity level at 80 percent. And different, too, from being surrounded by hundreds of acres of peanut plants and a nagging brother.

Dan used to love peanut butter as a kid. He thought it cool that his father grew the very nuts that made his sandwich filling for lunch. Now if he even smelled a hint of peanut butter, he became nauseated. All his life, Dan had worked his pop's peanut fields. He gathered it was his duty as a farmer's kid to help make the land profitable, to do his share of the work. A generational kind of thing. And of course, the peanut was the mark of a fine Virginia crop. Pop proudly sold his peanuts to the processing plants at Wakefield and received nice profits in return. Rob often remarked that Dan wouldn't have his iPod and laptop if not for their blessed peanuts. To Dan, he couldn't care less that the family icon was the Planters peanut man. All he wanted to do was get as far away from this place as possible. If only he didn't feel obligated to stay and keep the farm going. Pop always said he would rather work with his sons than hire outside help. He liked them by his side, tending to the operations. He was confident of their abilities. But Dan felt he was slowly being smashed into peanut butter with each passing day.

"As usual, you don't listen to a word I'm saying," Rob grumbled. "Pop ought to just tell you to leave."

Sounds good to me. If only he would. But he won't. Instead of answering, Dan hid behind the magazine. Rob stormed off. Dan read another paragraph then pitched the magazine onto the stand and stood to his feet. He liked the work he and Pop did in his early teens, renovating the two-story farmhouse built in the late nineteenth century. Those days were fun. He worked side by side with Pop, creating a home they could be proud of. Putting in wallboard. Making bookshelves. Redecorating his own personal place of refuge. At that time anything was better than working the fields and watching

Rob tend to the peanut plants as if they were his pals. In Dan's mind, peanut plants were akin to mosquitoes, sucking the lifeblood out of him.

With a halfhearted gesture, Dan moseyed on out to the yard where Pop was in the middle of showing Rob how to operate the new tractor he'd acquired. Instead of concentrating on the tractor, Dan imagined rafts, hiking equipment, a raging river, and adventure.

"Come on over, son, and let me show you how this works."

Dan shuffled over, staring into the sky, his thoughts higher than the fluffy clouds passing by, while his father explained the vehicle's operation.

"Give it a try, Dan."

"Huh?"

Rob burst out laughing. "I wouldn't unless you want him to wreck it."

"Excuse me, but I know how to operate a tractor," Dan retorted. He brushed past his snickering brother and climbed onto the narrow metal seat. Looking at the controls, he realized at once this machine was not the same as his father's old clunker. He engaged the engine, ignoring his father who tried to shout out the operating instructions above the loud noise. Dan put the gears in high range. The tractor lurched forward, heading at a fast clip toward a field of healthy green peanut plants. By the time he put his foot on the clutch, the tractor had succeeded in crushing a patch of plants.

Pop shook his head in dismay.

Rob hooted. "What did I tell you? He's not worth anything here."

"Both my sons are worth everything I have and more," Pop said, offering his hand to Dan.

Dan ignored the gesture. He jumped off the tractor to

the ground and promptly fell flat on his face in the field, squashing more tender plants. When he came to his feet, his clothes were plastered with dirt, including his new jeans. He strode off in a fury, kicking up a stone as he went, vowing to get out of here as soon as he could.

He flew into the house and headed for the shower. If there was one thing Dan couldn't stand anymore, it was the filth of a peanut field on him. Life itself had become one big pile of dirt, forever encrusted on his hands and clothing. At times it took an hour to scrub the dirt out of every crevice. The red clay of Virginia seemed permanently etched into his flesh.

Dan stayed in the shower for twenty minutes until he heard someone rap on the door. When he finally toweled off and dressed, Pop was waiting for him downstairs.

"Something bothering you, son?" he inquired. "You don't seem like yourself today."

Dan wanted so much to say what was going on in his heart. If only he could. He would let it all out—all the reasons he hated the farm and the idea of being the peanut man's son, and how life seemed to be on a dead-end road. There were places to see and things to do. He didn't want to find himself a permanent fixture in a field, listening to Rob complaining about his work habits and getting all the glory. If only Pop could understand that a man needed to get out and explore the world, to find his place and what he's meant to do.

Instead Dan lied, telling his father he was just fine and scooting off into the kitchen. Mom stood at the counter making pies. She spent most of her time in the kitchen, cooking up a storm to feed her three boys, as she called them. Dan never had a want for great food. Mom cooked up the best steaks, potatoes, cakes, and breads. She worked day and night to feed them well. Never once did he recall thanking her for the meals either—a thought that, for a moment, pricked his conscience. Then again, he worked his fingers to the bone on this farm of his father's. The reward, he supposed, was a good dinner to end a nondescript day.

He snitched some raw piecrust from the pastry cloth where she was rolling out the dough. He then planted a kiss on her cheek for good measure. "Hey, that's not good for you!" she exclaimed with a smile, then kissed him back.

"I know, like most stuff it seems." He opened the refrigerator, took out a plastic bowl, and began eating the casserole left from last night. He didn't care that it was ice cold. It was still good, with homemade noodles and chunks of chicken.

"I've been trying to find out what's bothering Dan here," Pop said to Mom. "He won't say a word."

"He's probably hungry. Look at how he's eating."

I'm hungry all right, he thought. Hungry for adventure, for a nice woman, for eating out with the boys, maybe even sharing in a few cold beers—though his godly parents would surely balk at the idea of their nice son drinking anything except milk and soda. He never told them how he went out once while they were away and bought a six-pack of beer. He took the six-pack, went up to his room, put on the loudest music he could, and drank all six cans. Having consumed little in the way of liquor in his life, those six cans on an empty stomach immediately made him woozy. He drank half a bottle of mouthwash, hoping to disguise his breath before realizing the mouthwash also contained alcohol. Finally he collapsed on the bed, telling everyone through the closed door that he was sick. His Christian parents never knew about the drinking escapade, or if they did, they said nothing.

And then there was Lenora, whom he met during a two-year

stint on the community college scene. Beautiful Lenora. Dark hair, fair skin. His parents disliked her. They said he shouldn't be dating a non-Christian, that her foul mouth and other points did not a match make. He said he was old enough to decide who he wanted to date. It was the only time he'd seen his father angry over his decision. As it was, time took care of the problem. Lenora captured another guy's heart, and they ended up marrying last year. And the college career ended soon after when he flunked out and ran out of money. Dan assumed his parents' prayers were answered, having him safely back on home turf, alone, unattached, and broke, to continue in the Mallory tradition of peanut keeping.

That was another thing that bothered him. His parents' praying and other religious habits. He went to church like a dutiful son should, but it meant little. His parents prayed constantly for him and his older brother. On occasion he overheard the praying, especially late at night when his parents were in the family room. They would sit together side by side with their hands clasped, offering long intercession for the family. Dan didn't want to admit it, but he felt those prayers calming him when life turned sour. Nor did he want to admit it when his father pointed out his call for salvation back at age thirteen, but how it meant little to him now. No doubt those prayers were acting like superglue, trying to keep his feet planted on this peanut farm and under a righteous umbrella. But inside, Dan remained restless, and he didn't know why. He just knew that if he didn't break away soon from all this, he'd turn as nutty as the legumes they grew.

"Now don't eat too much," Mom said with another smile, gently taking the container out of his hands. "I'm making one of your favorite meals tonight. Pot roast."

"Sounds good, Mom. You make the best." He strode out of

the house, the screen door banging shut behind him, only to stop short in the yard. Beyond the house lay the peanut fields. Rob was behind the wheel of the new tractor that pulled a cart, expertly driving it back and forth, hauling supplies dropped off by a delivery truck into the barn for storage. Dan ground his teeth. Rob was perfect at everything about farming. Dan would be perfect in his job, too, if he found a job to his liking. He took out the magazine he had rolled up and stuck in his back pocket after his shower. A wilderness adventure was more his style. Like rafting the wild Colorado River. Feasting on the great meals the rafting outfits cooked for dinner. Wearing all the newfangled sports clothes and sandals instead of jeans that smelled like cow dung and boots stained with the red clay of Virginia. Seeing the wild beauty of places like Arches National Park, unlike the fields of nothing around here. Oh how he wanted a new life. He swatted at a mosquito looking to take a bite out of his flesh. He wanted it bad.

"So what's going on, son?" a voice inquired.

Dan whirled to find his father behind him, peering at the magazine he held. He rolled it up quickly. "Nothing."

"Mind if I take a look?"

Dan reluctantly handed him the magazine. Now he would hear the proverbial lecture, how he should be thinking about the family and not chasing after some dream. Instead his father looked it over until he came to the back of the magazine where Dan had circled several ads for work as an adventure guide.

"Is this what you want to do?"

Dan blinked at the question he posed. He decided to answer just as succinctly. "Yes."

"Why? I didn't know you liked it so much. You only went rafting that one time, if I recall."

"I don't know. It was a blast the time I went. It's something completely different and in a different state. Something totally new."

Pop squinted at the fields and then looked at the barn where Rob was unloading supplies. "You really don't want to be a farmer, do you?"

Dan looked at his father. He thought for sure he would hear stories about how the peanut farm had been in the family for generations and that it was his duty to keep it going. "No. I can't stand it, Pop. I've tried to be happy, but this is not what I want to do. It's not for me. Rob is better at the farm stuff anyway. You don't need the both of us working here. He does everything."

"But I do need you, son. I need both my sons to make this place work. If you left, I would have to hire another helper."

"No, you wouldn't. Rob does it all. Look at what a great season you had last year while I was taking classes. He's a one-man show, all by himself."

"But look at us now, working side by side, making the farm happen with the people you love. It's knowing that together we can roll up our sleeves, work hard, and watch a harvest blessed by God. We can enjoy the fruit that comes with it. You have to admit there's been good fruit from working here in the past."

Dan couldn't argue with that. He had a nice Smartphone, and last year, a new laptop waiting for him at Christmas. But there was more to life than those things. There remained the constant nagging in his heart to go places. Here on the farm, he felt like life was passing him by. All the guys out West were having fun, and he was stuck shoveling manure and waiting for peanuts to form beneath the ground.

"So you have your heart set on being a river guide."

"Maybe. I need to get my feet wet first. See what the possibilities are out there. Try my hand at something different."

"Well, I can't force you to stay here. If you want to leave, it's your decision." He began to walk away.

"Hey, Pop? If I decide to leave, I'll need some money to settle down with. You said that we were earning money as we worked here. I'm sure I've earned something these past fifteen years."

"You mean the money that's in the trust fund I set up for each of you boys?"

Dan nodded without reservation. "I need money. Can't move and get a place to rent without money."

Pop sighed long and hard. "I'll take your share out of the bank if that's what you want. I hope you've prayed about this and you're certain this is what God wants you to do. You realize that once you use up the money, that's it. There won't be anything left."

Nothing to it, Dan thought gleefully. *With the kind of money these guys must be making in the adventure business, I'll be able to return the favor and then some.* Excitement surged through him at the possibility. "Sure, I understand. But I don't plan to waste it, Pop. I'll be making money, too, so it won't matter."

Pop looked at him, his mouth open to say something, then nodded. The conversation had ended, and Dan had won. He smiled to himself. This had gone better than he ever could have hoped or dreamed. He figured Pop would fight him all the way, but he'd acquiesced as if it were nothing at all. Surely this must mean it was the right thing to do.

Dan grabbed the magazine flier out of his pocket and waved it like a banner for the world to see. "Moab, Utah, here I come!"

two

What's on your mind?

Jolene. . .*is tired of red rocks, heat waves, muddy water, and irate customers.*

Jolene, or Jo, as she liked to be called, hit the ENTER button on the keyboard and watched the statement appear on the "wall." She sat back in her seat, staring at her avatar—her cheerful face parked inside a raft, of course. What other picture would she have on her Facebook page? And what other link would she have posted except one for Red Canyon Adventures of Moab, owned by her cousin, Todd.

Now she reread the words she'd posted. How cynical they seemed. Thankfully Todd rarely accessed his Facebook page, or he would wonder why she wrote such a thing. And he'd make some remark, too, about how a posting like that could hurt his business. Jo never shared her feelings with her cousin these days. She'd come out here from the East to help but found herself being scorched instead, just like the fiery red rocks under the intense Utah sun. If he knew her thoughts, he would decide she was suffering another round of PMS—of which on those days he told her to take the day off. If only he knew everything. But guys don't usually notice things like that. Instead they loved food, electronic gadgets, a girl, a good time.

"I'd like to book a one-day trip, please."

Jo continued to stare at the computer screen until she heard a loud "Ahem." She looked up to see a rather plump man with sunglasses attached to a colorful band encircling his throat. Beside him stood his equally rotund wife. They looked like typical vacationers to Moab. Probably came here in their RV from who knows where, parked it in one of the expensive RV parks north of town, and now wanted to experience all that the area had to offer.

"How can I help you?"

"We want to book a one-day rafting trip for two."

Jo tried not to snap her gum like some teen bored by the routine and the customer. "Let's see. We have room on a raft of ten leaving at 8:30 a.m. tomorrow."

"We want to arrange our own private rafting trip. Just the two of us."

Jo looked at him. "We usually like to place you with other passengers. And it adds to the trip, sharing it with others." She already had that icky feeling that this was not going to be a pleasant encounter. Another irate customer who wanted his way would further substantiate her posting on her Facebook wall.

The man went on to explain how he'd promised Tootsie—she guessed that was the woman's name—her own boat ride down the Colorado.

"I'll ask Todd what he can do for you. He's the manager." She picked up the walkie-talkie and turned away, not wishing to look anymore at the man's irritated face. She put forth the question.

Todd answered.

"Okay, thanks." She turned back to the guy. "Todd will take you on a private excursion, but it will cost extra."

He didn't seem to care but plunked down a debit card. It didn't surprise her that Todd had agreed. He always had dollar signs for pupils in his eyes these days. How Jo wished she could convince him there were more important things in life than making money. Like having God in the picture. But these days, everyone was looking for money and making it the only way they knew how.

The man bustled over with his and her bottles of suntan lotion, energy bars, and drinks. Jo rang up the purchases, thinking about the time when she first tried to share God with Todd. "Please don't get into that religious stuff, Jolene. I've been doing just fine without God for twenty-six years."

Jo wondered how she ever existed without God now that she knew Him. Scratch that. Even a single moment. She'd found out the hard way she couldn't. . .which made her think of something different to write on the wall of her Facebook page. When the couple left, she returned to the Internet and deleted the last post. She entered her favorite verse from Philippians. *I can do everything through Him who gives me strength.* She smiled at those faith-filled words that infused her spirit with strength. If there was one thing she needed right now, it was a zap of faith. And maybe a new lease on life.

"Wow, it's great to be finally here. This place is amazing."

Another bright and cheery customer. Though she shouldn't complain. Business was tough enough with the fierce competition between the numerous rafting companies here in Moab. She looked up and this time allowed her gum to snap at the college-aged guy who wandered in, no doubt seeking the wildest rafting experience they had to offer. Jo already had the sales pitch on her lips, ready to recommend the two-day excursion into Cataract Canyon with Class IV and V rapids. Her fingers curled around the brochure.

He strode up to the counter with confidence oozing out of every pore. He wore expensive shades that could use a fancy band to hold them in place. Jo looked over to see the eyeglass bands sadly lacking on the display rack, including her favorite color—purple. She made a mental note to remind Todd to reorder a few more. "I've got just the trip for you. Cataract Canyon." She launched into her sales pitch.

The man whipped off his shades and gently pressed a finger against her lips. The contact made her leap to her feet. How dare he touch her like that! And how dare she find it exciting for a brief moment. She stepped back and shook her head as if to ward off the thought.

"Sorry. I didn't mean anything. I just wanted to quiet you for a second so I can explain why I'm here. I'm looking for a job, not a trip."

"We already did our hiring back in the winter. Sorry." She didn't bother to add that Todd was thinking of cutting back on employees, as profits had been slipping with the wavering economy.

"Well, I see there's tons of rafting companies around here. Any you know of that might be hiring river guides?

"You know the rivers around here?"

He thought for a moment. "I'm a fast learner."

She laughed. How typical—boast first for an attention-grabber then admit later that he knows nothing about what he wants to do. "There's a lot to learn about running a raft down the Colorado. You can't just walk off the street and expect to paddle a boat safely with paying customers on board. And you need to be licensed by the state before you can conduct a trip. Do you have any experience?"

"Well, I went on a rafting trip in West Virginia, on the Gauley River. Ever hear of it? Some of the wildest rapids you've ever seen."

"What class were they?"

His forehead furrowed. "Oh, the best class. Top of the class, if you know what I mean. First-rate white water." He winked.

Jo wondered if he was joking around with her or really didn't know the first thing about rafting. "Well, you can check with Todd to see if he could use an extra hand. He might need someone to help with cooking on the family trips. Driving the bus. Or organizing gear. But honestly, we're rather tight right now on our budget. Like everyone else these days, we're cutting back."

"I'd rather paddle a boat than fix a meal."

"I know, but you have to start somewhere. Most of the trips we do include either a picnic lunch or full meals for the overnight trips. So you need to know it all. We serve some of the best food, too, I might add." She wanted to boast about her involvement in that aspect, helping Todd discover that serving customers satisfying meals brought them back, or in the least, served as a way to spread a good word about their company. "Did you know our meals were rated one of the top of the companies here in Moab? I used to help with the cooking, but now I mostly man the reservations desk."

He leaned over the counter, his rugged face with a five o'clock shadow and breath scented with peppermint a bit too close for comfort. "And I'll bet you're the best cook around. That's why you won the awards."

"I can charbroil a steak quite well, thanks. And I make fabulous brownies." She felt her cheeks warm as his hazel-colored eyes leveled on her and then began tracing her facial features.

"Sounds great. How about having me over for dinner so I can taste some of your cooking?"

She snapped her fingers. "Wouldn't you know it, I'm booked solid." She thought about her social calendar, which included the Internet and gathering with church friends Wednesday nights. Besides, the guy was getting a little too friendly for comfort. "Well, if you're willing to do some tasks like cooking, equipment handling, stuff like that, Todd might be interested."

"I suppose that's better than nothing. I have plenty of money to start up here anyway. Which reminds me, can you suggest a place to rent? Anyplace will do, just until I get settled and have time to look for a house."

"You can check the classifieds in the local paper for apartments and rooms for rent."

"Okay, thanks." He paused. "Do you know when Todd might be back?"

"Not sure. He had to make a run this afternoon. Should be back by six."

"Six, huh? Guess I have time then to get acquainted with the town. Maybe you can take a lunch break and show me around. It's getting to be that hour, and I'm hungry."

Jo looked at the clock and the hands moving toward the noon hour. A break would be nice, even if it was with an overly eager guy who had no idea what he was doing or where he was going in life. "Okay. I can get Christine to cover."

"Super. Know any good places to eat?"

"I like the Moab Diner. It has great Mexican food."

"Mexican food at a diner? This I've got to see."

Jo felt like a mom ready to escort her eager son. She'd never seen such excitement in someone who couldn't wait to see what Moab had to offer. If only she could tell him how dull this life would soon become. But she supposed someone eager to run the river would find it all exciting. Maybe if she had stuck it out with the camping and cooking part of the deal and not demoted herself to a desk job, life would be more interesting. Though that was her fault. Todd needed someone capable to man the desk. And she agreed to do it. Besides, *godliness with contentment is great gain.* Wow, did she need to work on the contentment part of life. Like this guy, who seemed content just to be here in Moab. And here she was, contemplating how to get away from Moab.

They arrived at the Moab Diner with its red plastic booths and granite-colored tables, a hangout for many of the rafting guys. She and the guy quickly nabbed a seat. To her dismay, she spotted their competitor Chris Rhodes and some friends at another table. She wondered why he wasn't out on the river today. She hoped he didn't notice her. That's all she needed to top her day.

"So what's good here?" he asked. "I suppose the tacos."

Jo kept her eye trained on Chris. So far so good. With the empty plates before them, she hoped they were about ready to leave. She still recalled the painful episode that erupted between Chris and Todd over a huge group looking to hire a rafting company for a special weekend excursion. Todd did everything he could to land the contract, even spreading a rumor about Chris and his company, which Todd thought was legit and used it to his advantage. When Chris got wind of it, nasty words flew and nearly fists as well.

"You look like something's on your mind," the guy interrupted. "Hey, do you realize we haven't even introduced ourselves? I'm Dan Mallory."

Jo turned her attention to him. "Jolene Davidson. But I like to go by Jo."

"Jolene. Nice southern name, like from Tennessee. Or Georgia."

"Well, if it isn't the Red Canyon Adventures co-conspirator," came a voice.

Chris had spotted her. *Super.* Jo tried to focus her gaze on the menu, which turned blurry.

"I'm still amazed your cousin can sleep nights after the stunt he pulled last month," Chris went on.

"I had nothing to do with it," she said quickly.

"Sure, sure." Chris then looked at Dan. "And who's this? Another one you managed to con into an adventure? Or into the company?"

"I'm Dan, fresh from the East," Dan said, offering his hand. "I'm looking for a job here in a rafting company."

"Well, if you want my advice, don't work for Red Canyon Adventures. Their only adventure seems to be spreading lies and running everyone else out of business."

"It wasn't an out-and-out lie. You were rumored to have a salmonella problem," Jo said in a low voice.

Chris stared with daggers in his eyes.

"There's nothing wrong with making a profit as long as it's honest work," Dan added.

An eyebrow raised on Chris's face. "There's a big difference when that profit comes from unethical means. I'm sure Jolene can fill you in. And for your information, we were cleared of that salmonella thing."

"Hey, are you by chance looking for workers?" Dan interrupted.

"Nope, we're not. Sorry." He then returned to Jo. "Tell Todd I don't forget things easily, Jolene. And he ought to be making apologies real quick, 'cause time's running out." He gave one last steely-eyed look before whirling about and leaving.

"Wow, I had no idea you companies were out to spill each other's blood," Dan said, his eyes wide. "What's he talking about?"

"My cousin likes to make money, and he got the group Chris wanted. Todd will do whatever's necessary to make things work to his advantage, even if he has to tell a tall tale. I mean, there was a rumor that Chris's company had an outbreak of salmonella poisoning, but like Chris said, it was never proven. Because of it, Todd got Chris's groups."

"Not a good idea to spread a rumor unless it's true," Dan said slowly as if thinking on his own words. "I mean, I'll admit I sometimes fibbed or took shortcuts, but I always ended up getting burned by it. It never seems to work out in the end."

"I wish Todd would learn that lesson." She suddenly considered the idea of Dan joining their company. Maybe it would be good for her cousin to have a guy who had some moral backing to him. One who might be able to point out questionable activities before it was too late and they all suffered as a result. Like giving people trips they didn't want or taking away groups from other companies by telling everyone their food was bad or spreading other rumors. Todd might listen to a guy over her, not that he hadn't listened to her past objections. But if Todd got a guy's take on things, it might work out for the better. "Hey Dan, if I got Todd to interview you, would you consider working for our company? I mean, you weren't spooked by what Chris said, were you?"

"Are you kidding? 'Course not. I'll take what I can get. That's why I'm here. I mean, I'd rather not end up the official company cook. I would really like to help guide a boat or something."

"Well, you need training, you know. But I'll see what he can do for you."

The waitress ventured up to take their orders. Dan took the initiative, ordering the specialty—the Navajo taco. Jo wasn't sure she could handle the food right now with the painful twinge in her stomach, made more intense by all this commotion. But God had divinely arranged for this meeting, maybe to bring back to the rafting company some semblance of virtue that had been lacking. She decided on a Mexican stir-fry, then returned her attention to Dan. "So what kind of shortcuts have you taken in the past?" she wondered aloud.

Dan looked at her in surprise. "Why are you asking me that?"

"It's good to know a person's background. Call it a background check, so to speak. And to make sure you're not bringing any surprises into the company."

"Look, I came here with a clean slate. No police record or anything, I promise. Even got that one speeding ticket cleared up before I left the state. The only employer I worked for was my pop, and I know he would vouch for me. Maybe. I mean, sometimes you take shortcuts on the home front, like Pop tells you to do something, and suddenly you get a call on the cell phone and forget to complete the project. That sort of thing."

"So you worked for your father?"

"Yeah, we raise peanuts for a living, if you can believe it. How's that for a nutty profession?" He laughed so long and loud, Jo had to wonder if something else lay hidden behind the laughter. She'd known many people who hid some untold pain behind a joke or laugh. "Now you see why I wanted to come here."

"Well, this isn't all that glamorous either. If you like broiling days and river water sloshing all over you and customers who aren't always friendly. . ."

"Are you kidding? Sounds great. Anything is better than watching peanut plants grow. Believe me."

To Jo, the idea of working with plants, waiting for the fruit of the earth to come forth, even if it was sight unseen in the ground, seemed like a nice change compared to red rocks, hot sun, and trying to work through the idiosyncrasies of people in the rafting business. Maybe they should switch jobs. "How about I go work on your dad's peanut farm and you can work for Todd," she suggested with a laugh. "It will be our own reality show. I'd love to watch plants grow. And I like honey-roasted peanuts. After a while, all these rocks can get to you. Makes you feel like you're living on Mars or something."

Dan laughed, too, this time in a friendly manner that sent warmth radiating through her. "Pop would sure love to meet you—and Mom, too, but then I wouldn't get to know everything about you." At that moment their meals arrived, the scent of cumin and cilantro rising into the air. "And I'll need lessons in cooking, if that's where I end up. You can show me how to do a steak up right and make me a first-class Iron Chef like Bobby Flay."

Jo bent her head to pray and set the future in God's hands. "And help us know, dear God, if you wish Dan to be a part of our rafting company. In Jesus' name, amen." When she looked up, Dan sat there, hazel eyes wide open, fork in hand, ready to take a bite. *Okay, so this guy is different.* He certainly had enthusiasm. Maybe he can help put the business on the right footing. Fresh blood in the company, so to speak. New life. And she prayed, maybe new hope, too. The business sure needed it. She could use some of it as well.

three

So far Dan could not be more pleased with how everything was working out. It had been smooth sailing from the moment he arrived in Moab and then fell into company with the very attractive co-proprietor of Red Canyon Adventures. Jo got him a job as soon as she introduced him to her cousin Todd. Not that he cared much when she mentioned he would cook. But if the cooking part got his foot in the door, or rather, in a raft, he would take it from there and become the captain of his own ship in no time. With training, that is.

Dan lingered before the mirror on his first official day in the rafting business, gelling his hair, checking out the new tight-fitting polyester shirt, board shorts, river sandals, and of course, shades. He looked the part, even if he didn't have the slightest idea what he was doing. But in this game, looks and confidence mattered. It worked well in sealing this deal when he put the charm on Jo and snagged a job. How he wanted to call home and gloat over the fact with mighty bro and Pops.

He did call once, letting the family know he'd arrived safely in Moab. Pop said little. He received a text message from Rob who told him how Mom was in his bedroom looking over some of his belongings that he'd left behind. Dan thought about that for a few moments before deleting the message. He loved Mom and missed her fine cooking. The more he thought about the family back home the worse he felt, so he chose not to think about it. Mom would pray anyway, and that would make her feel better. And when she learned how happy he was here, how many bucks he was making, and how life was sweet for him in Moab, she would be okay with his decision. And maybe he could even invite her and Pop to come out, and he'd take them on a rafting trip. He'd cook Pop a steak the way he liked it. And they would know without a doubt this is where he was meant to be.

But all the niceties still didn't make things feel right. Somewhere deep inside, he had a nagging doubt. He didn't know what to make of it either. Like a black cloud trying to dull the sunshine, of which there was no lack in this place. In fact, the other items he bought besides the clothes were a bottle of heavy-duty waterproof sunscreen and a hat. But once he thought of the action to come today—his first trip on the river to see all that there was to see—the doubt fled. Maybe it was just nerves.

He hooked up his iPod and made tracks. No way did he want to be late on his first day. Hopping inside his newly purchased used Jeep—he wished he could afford a new one but didn't want to use up all his money—he peeled off down the road, gunning the engine for effect. Ah, life was good.

Suddenly he saw the flashing strobe lights of a police car in his rearview mirror. "Oh, man," he mumbled, looking at the speedometer, wondering how fast he'd been going. He pulled over to the shoulder.

The officer sauntered up as if he were used to pulling over beach guys in their red Jeeps. "I need to see your license and registration, please."

"I have a Virginia license. The registration hasn't arrived yet. I just got here and recently bought this Jeep."

"Hmm. Not a great way to be introduced to Moab's speed limit of thirty. Especially doing fifty."

Dan blew out a sigh. "Any chance you can let me off with

a warning? I'm on my way to my job. It's my first day. And I guess I need to get used to the speed limit around here. And this new Jeep. Too many new things."

The officer looked as if he'd heard all these arguments before. He said nothing but walked back to his vehicle to perform a security check. Dan tapped his fingers on the steering wheel and looked at his watch, realizing he was about to be late for his first day on the job. And he was about to see his insurance skyrocket with another ticket. This was not good. Life was bad. He should've skipped the gel routine this morning and given himself extra time.

After a few minutes the officer returned. "I'll let you off with a warning. But the speed limit in town is thirty."

"Thank you so much, Officer. And if you ever want a rafting trip, Red Canyon Adventures has the best! And I'll make sure they give you a discount."

The officer cocked an eyebrow, shook his head, and returned to his car. "Thank you, God," Dan said loudly and took off, this time making sure the speedometer did not inch anywhere near the thirty-mile-per-hour mark. He should be thanking God for a lot of things these days. After all, he had a nice apartment, his fine red Jeep to cruise around in, a rafting job, a friend in Jo. He smiled when he thought of her. She was a neat girl who loved life, even if she seemed a little worn out by it. Maybe he could lift her mood. He would infuse enthusiasm into her dull and dreary life. If only she knew what a dull life really was. . .like driving a tractor in a peanut field. She would thank her lucky stars she lived here in Moab.

He made it to the center with a minute to spare. There he found the boss, Todd, giving directions to the other employees. Paying customers, outfitted in everything from short shorts to one in a pair of jean shorts that hung to his kneecaps, stood ready to embark on their journey down the Colorado. Dan ventured forward and greeted everyone. "Hi, I'm Dan Mallory."

"Nothing like getting here at the last minute," Todd noted.

"Sorry. I'm not used to the speed limit."

"Sylvester pull you over?"

Dan laughed loudly, thinking of Sylvester the "puddy tat," according to Tweety. "Don't know, but whoever it was let me off with a warning. You have a real friendly and forgiving town here."

Todd nodded. "Okay, we're gonna pile into the bus and head over to the loading area. Next time, Dan, I need you here an hour earlier to help load up the boats and other gear."

"Yeah, you can't be showing up anytime you want," another guy added.

Dan detected the sarcasm in the voice and wondered if he might be in trouble. "Sorry, I didn't know that. I'll be early next time."

Todd looked at his clipboard. "Your job today is lunch since you don't have training for anything else. I assume you know how to make sandwiches."

"Like PB and J?" Dan again laughed, only to find Todd and the other guy staring at him in displeasure. "Sorry, that was lame. You see, I used to work on a peanut farm back home."

"Boy, you are from the back hills of the East," the other guy murmured.

Todd went on to explain Dan's job for the day, taking care of the lunch preparations. Just then, Dan noticed Jo walk out, carrying a large cooler. He and Todd went to help her load it onto the bus.

"You need to get here earlier," she told him. "Travis was having a meltdown that you hadn't shown up and he was stuck with all the work of loading the gear."

Dan nodded. "So that's his name. Better than saying, 'Hey you.' Yeah, I already got bawled out about it. Sorry." He hoped for a smile but instead saw a grim expression on her face. He couldn't see her eyes behind the sunglasses that shielded them. "So what's on the lunch menu?"

"Sandwiches, fruit, cookies, lemonade. The usual." She paused. "Oops, that's right, you don't know the usual."

"And here I thought we'd be cooking steaks."

"That's on overnight trips. But hang around long enough, and you'll get to do that, too."

"Honestly, what I really want to do is be a river guide. Wonder when Todd will let me do that?"

"Oh, he might introduce you to it today, just for kicks. You have to train anyway on the river for a solid three weeks. Then pass a test."

"So I might do something today? Wow, I thought I'd have to be at this game forever before I'd get a chance to man the helm."

"This is not a difficult section of the river. He'll probably have Travis give you some pointers on the calmest section. It's a perfect place to learn the ropes."

Dan hoped that they would also be entering calmer waters where he might be able to learn more about Jo. "You're coming today, right?"

"Nope. Someone's got to hold down the cash register and book the trips."

"I guess so." He thought about asking if she wanted to grab a burger afterward, but he heard Todd's impatient voice inquiring if the food was ready. Jo and Dan hurried over to load the back end of the bus with the fixings for lunches, along with the dry bags. "Make sure you put the food like the chips, cookies, and rolls into the dry bags before you load them onto the rafts," Jo instructed, holding up the stiff waterproof bags used on the rafts.

"Wish me luck," Dan said, eyeing her lips when he said it. *Get a hold of yourself, Dan the man. It's too soon to be begging a good-luck kiss. You just met her three days ago. Give it time.* But her lips looked tantalizing all the same. He wished he had her along to help him. He nearly suggested to Todd that an attractive sandwich maker by his side might be a nice addition to his first day on the job. He dismissed it when Todd and Travis climbed on board the bus. He followed suit.

"Have a good time," Jo said with a smile.

It was a pleasant send-off, not as nice as a kiss would be, but nice all the same. He let her sweet words soak into his withered being that was now getting even more withered from the intense heat. "How hot does it get here?" he asked Travis when they settled into their seats.

Travis didn't answer for a long moment. He then said, "Hot."

What was this guy's problem? He must still be mad that Dan arrived late and he was stuck with the work. "Okay, hot as in what?"

"Gets to a hundred plus. Even in the shade."

"Wow. We get some days like that in Virginia. But it was always so humid, too."

"You don't get that here. It's dry heat. Low humidity levels." Travis then pulled out a racing car magazine. Dan frowned in contempt. Travis would have to be reading a NASCAR rag. His brother Rob ate and breathed NASCAR. Rob sometimes went to the speedway in Richmond or the one in North Carolina somewhere to catch the action. He loved the stuff.

Dan pushed the irritation aside to glance behind him at the assorted customers eager to taste a river adventure. They came in all sizes and with various backgrounds. One of the women didn't look too pleased about the whole deal, judging by the way she sat tense in her seat, wrinkles creasing her young face. She had frosted hair and big hoop earrings. Her boyfriend had his meaty arm hooked around her as if trying to soothe her nerves.

"It's gonna be a blast, sweetie. You'll love it."

"If I fall out, I'm suing," she told him flatly.

"If you fall out, I get to rescue you. And it will be great."

She wiggled out of his grasp and folded her arms in a huff. "If I fall out I'll sue, and I'll drop you, too."

Dan had to smirk. There were parts of this job he hadn't anticipated, like the clientele. He never was much of a people observer, but this was already proving to be quite entertaining.

The bus hissed and groaned for the hour ride through a pristine area of genuine Utah wilderness, with tall cliffs and rock formations bordering the river. Finally it came to a stop at the drop-off area. Several other rafting outfitters were already at work, readying their prospective clients and boats. Dan noticed the guy, Chris, from the restaurant the other day. Thankfully the guy didn't say anything but was busy with his own outfit. After the conflict in the restaurant, Dan didn't care to see more blood spilled here. But so far everything looked peaceful.

Dan helped Travis and the other employees unload the boats while Todd gathered the group together for a quick safety lesson. Each was equipped with a life preserver or what Todd called a PFD or personal flotation device. Dan wondered what the guy wearing the jean shorts would do when his clothing became waterlogged. At least it was plenty warm today; they might actually dry. Already the perspiration was rolling down Dan's face. He wanted to ask about drinking water, but Travis was barking at him for not having the dry bags of food ready.

"It would be nice if someone filled me in on what to do," Dan said.

"Jolene said you knew everything about rafting trips. I didn't think we'd have to go back to grade school."

Oh man. Me and my bloated ego. Dan remembered how he'd tried to sell himself to Jo with all that talk of rafting in West Virginia, when he'd only been on one trip. He was eating his own words. "Well, every rafting company does things differently, so I want to make sure I don't mess things up."

Travis seemed to accept this explanation and began to explain their routine for the trip. Dan felt better about it all when Todd signaled to them. Dan buckled on his PFD and climbed in with Todd and half the company, which included the nervous woman with the large earrings and her manhandling boyfriend. Travis skippered the other boat with the remaining passengers and the food.

Pure excitement pulsated through Dan as they each picked up paddles, ready to attack the river. The passengers all talked excitedly as they took off down the Colorado. An azure sky reflected in the bounding waters. The rocky formations of cliffs and spirals, painted dark orange and red, fascinated him. Dan began to learn the names of the formations. Fisher Towers. Castle Valley. Even one that looked like a church with rock people standing before it. They stopped at one point on the river to play a game with the paddles and take a nature walk. Dan had never felt such a thrill in all his life. To witness all this before his very eyes after months of reading about it in magazines seemed too good to be true. Rob would be jealous if he could see him now. *The whole family would be jealous*, Dan thought. This was life at its best, and he was being paid for it. Nothing could be better.

The boats drifted easily over a few rapids in the river to the delight of the passengers. Everyone seemed to be enjoying it except earring girl who complained to her boyfriend that the up and down motion of the boat was making her sick. "Just have fun," he told her. "This is great!"

"I don't think this is fun at all. I just know I'm gonna fall out of this thing."

Dan shook his head, wishing that she, like the others, could put a smile on her face, relax, and enjoy the splendid Utah scenery. He certainly was and couldn't wait to help man the boat later on.

❧

Dan had just finished arranging the meats and cheeses in semicircles on plates, complete with snippets of parsley for decoration, when Todd ventured up. "Hey, that looks awesome, Dan. You look like a regular chef, arranging everything."

"Thanks to Mom. She liked to put on these lunches at church and always made sure everything looked good." For a moment he became lost in thought, thinking of Mom at those church functions and how she wanted everything to be perfect. Dan knew she only wanted to bless others and make them feel special. Could some of her be rubbing off on him, even out here in Utah?

When the lunch was ready, the guests gathered to make sandwiches. Dan looked on, pleased with himself as everyone commented on the fine spread. "Yo! Having fun yet?" he asked earring girl as she helped herself to the pasta salad.

She looked at him in surprise. "I guess. Bobby here tells

me this afternoon we're going to another beach area for some swimming and sunbathing. Know anything about it?"

"Well, uh. . ." Dan looked over at Todd. "I'm sure we are. I'm rather new here, so I'm just learning about this trip myself. But so far, it's been great."

"Yeah," she said before moving on to the plates filled with cookies. When everyone had been served, Todd, Travis, and Dan fixed themselves sandwiches and found a place to eat. Travis immediately complained about his raft and how the people refused to listen to instructions when it came to paddling.

"I've got a decent group," Todd remarked. "How about I switch with you, Travis, and you man my boat. You can show Dan some of the technique. This stretch of the river is perfect for learning some basics."

"I thought Dan was hired to cook."

Dan opened his mouth to object, only to find Todd coming to the rescue. "I could use a substitute guide, so the quicker we teach him, the quicker we can put him on a boat if we need to."

Dan tried to eat, but the expectation within him grew by the moment. Here Jo had given him tales of doom and gloom stuck in a chef's apron and hat. Instead, Todd was talking about him skippering his own boat. Was God doing things for him or what? Was God happy that he'd taken his inheritance and abandoned the family to go do his own thing? *Where did that thought come from?*

"Something up?" Todd asked him.

"No, no, just glad to be learning about rafting. That's why I came here."

"Well, I like your enthusiasm. And if the attention you gave to the lunch is anything like you will give to rafting, you're gonna do just fine."

Dan ate the rest of his sandwich with gusto, all the while thanking dear old Mom and her church luncheons for helping him out. He owed her a *Life Is Good* T-shirt. He'd seen that saying on shirts inside the store. But honestly, he owed her a whole lot more than he was willing to give.

❧

"Don't worry about it."

But Dan did worry about it, big-time. He sat on the bus, trying to avoid earring girl and her boyfriend who were likely staring at his back with daggers in their eyes. Okay, so his first time at the helm of the raft wasn't the best. He was told this was an easy stretch of river. How did he know there was a rock hidden under the water? Like he had X-ray vision or something. Who put it there anyway?

"I can't believe you didn't see it," Travis yelled at him. "You have to look at the water and the way it's flowing to see the obstacles and alert the passengers. You could clearly see how the current was making a vee around the rock."

When the raft sideswiped the rock, the motion sent everyone lurching. And suddenly earring girl was in the frothy river. She screamed, frantically waving her hands as if she were about to be swallowed up, even though the water was only waist deep. To make matters worse, her boyfriend sat in the boat and laughed. Travis held out a paddle to assist her back into the raft. Then to cap it off, she moaned how she'd sacrificed one of her precious earrings to the deep.

"Dan, are you hearing me?" Todd said.

"Yeah, sure."

"These things happen. It's not the first time, nor will it be the last. Passengers fall out. It's part of the river. That's why they wear a PFD and are taught what to do if they fall overboard."

Dan glanced at the rear of the bus to see earring girl and her red face. "She looks pretty mad. But she didn't help matters. I mean, she was leaning over the side of the boat already when it hit. Something about losing an earring."

"Don't worry about it, okay?"

Dan was happy that Todd seemed to be rooting for him. He felt certain after such apparent ineptness he'd be shown his way to the company exit. Especially after the big deal Travis made over it.

When they arrived back in Moab, Dan felt as if he had just completed an all-day marathon. His legs ached, and his arms even more so. His face felt as if it were on fire, and he had a pounding headache to boot. Inside the store he grabbed a cold bottle of water out of a refrigerated case and began gulping it down.

"Yo! You'll have to tell me what you took," said a sweet voice from across the way.

He looked over to find Jo tidying up the shirt rack.

"I have to know what you took out of the case so I can mark it down as employee compensation," she explained.

"I'll pay for it," Dan said.

"You don't have to. Just let me know. I mean, you can't walk out with merchandise, but you can take a drink and an energy bar now and then."

"Thanks." He had to admit Jo was a pleasing sight after this mixed-up day that had seen him go from exultation to exasperation.

She went to the cash register to begin signing out for the day. "You look bad. Got a nasty sunburn, too. You need to wear more sunscreen. That's some of our primary instruction to the customers. Wear sunscreen and drink plenty of water."

"I feel bad. As for the sunscreen, I remembered everything

else but forgot to put that on today." He leaned across the counter, feeling very weary indeed.

She gave him a sympathetic look. "Better grab a tube of aloe vera there. You can pay me for that. And would you be interested in stopping for ice cream after work?"

Dan immediately straightened. "Thanks. That'd be awesome."

"Just have to finish up. Be right back."

Dan waited with as much patience as he could muster, downing the rest of his drink. He took the tube of aloe vera and left the money on the counter, then applied the gooey blue gel to his burned face.

When Jo returned, she was carrying her purse, which was shaped like a small backpack. "Todd's gonna inventory out. He said you did fine today. The lunch was awesome." She took the money for the aloe vera and put it in the cash register.

"Thanks." Dan followed her into the hot sunshine of Moab that made his face and eyes hurt. "I guess if you can call running the raft into a rock fine."

"Oh, rafts hit obstacles all the time. They bounce."

"Yeah, but it bounced a little too much and earring girl got tossed out. She wasn't happy."

Jo laughed with a sound that warmed his sunburned soul. Oh, how he would love to curl his arm around her and soak up some of her sweetness. But he kept his arms to himself.

They entered the ice cream shop where Jo ordered them both extra large twist cones. "We'll have to eat in here. Outside they'll melt into a puddle in about five minutes." She led the way to two seats in the corner.

"Someone should do a test to see how long it takes for an extra large twist cone to melt in one-hundred-degree weather."

Jo laughed, licking away at the ice cream. Dan watched in spite of himself until he felt stickiness on his fingers and saw his ice cream already melting. He began taking big bites.

"Slow down, or you'll end up with a brain freeze."

"That would be all right. My head is hot enough as it is. At least my headache is better." He paused. "I just wish I hadn't rammed that boat into a rock. Everything was going so good. Todd really liked how I'd set up the lunch. And he's all interested in me becoming a substitute guide soon."

"Really? Then you did have a good day, even with the bump on the rock."

"If Travis would only be cool about things. I think he has it in for me as the newbie in all this."

Jo shrugged. "We were all new once. But don't let it get to you, Dan. You'll fit in just fine, and pretty soon you'll be guiding a trip with the best of them."

Dan was liking Jo more and more—and after only three days filled with lunch, ice cream, conversation, and laughter. He wanted so much to call her his girlfriend. Once again, he had to tell himself to slow it down. But maybe she was thinking the same thing, that she wanted him for her boyfriend. She didn't let on that she did. He would like to ask her and make it official. But he couldn't have everything he wanted in less than a week. An awesome job and a girlfriend to boot. Could he?

"You look like something's on your mind."

"I. . .uh, I'm happy to have a friend. When you're new in town, a friend is awesome."

"It's important. Friends make things better. And so can ice cream when you've had a tough day. I get a cone whenever I've had a tough day." She paused as if lost in her own thoughts.

"Has today been a tough day?"

"No, it's been pretty good, actually."

Dan was liking this more and more. He'd give it a few more days, tops. Jo was sure to be in his relationship status on Facebook. He hoped.

four

Jo couldn't help but feel compassion for Dan, even if he was brash at times and thought a bit too much of himself. Seeing him with his face burned that first day and looking as if he had run a marathon—it must be that motherly feeling creeping up in her. Though Jo could hardly think of motherly things at her age. Twenty-three years wasn't exactly a teenybopper, but neither was she old enough to think like a mother. She was just the age to enjoy life as a single person, though at times it proved challenging. At least Dan's arrival added some zip. He kept her on her toes when she needed to explain simple protocol. The other evening he'd stopped by the store asking for advice, claiming he needed to know all the ins and outs of this place if he was going to fit in. And other things, too—like handling irate customers such as earring girl, as he called her. Jo had to admit she admired his tenacity.

Jo entered the gear room that evening to sort out the PFDs left behind from the day's trips. Besides motherhood, there was another thing she wasn't looking forward to. Cleaning up after everyone. If the husband wasn't going to at least pitch in on a few of these assorted duties, life would be a struggle. But, then again, if he arrived home with a vase of red tulips—she missed seeing tulips blooming in Moab—and a box of those new candy-coated mint-chocolate candies, she would be in heaven, and all the mediocre jobs in the world would not sway her happy mood.

A few swear words echoing into the storeroom now sent her whirling. Travis was delivering a fresh set of wet gear, which he dumped on the floor. He swore again until his gaze rested on Jo.

"Do you mind?" she said. "We're trying to run a family business."

"We're in the storeroom, for crying out loud! And that guy Todd hired doesn't know what he's doing."

Uh-oh. Travis was complaining about Dan again. Poor Dan, who only wanted to do what's right. "What did Dan do this time?"

"We had him on dinner duty last night, and he burned the steaks. You know how much beef costs? Then another guy wanted his rare. Dan looked like he was going to be sick and refused to cook it that way. I had to do it. The guy's crazy. He doesn't belong with this outfit."

"He just needs some more training. We all had to go through training, Travis. Even you. I'll go next time on the overnighter and teach him the ropes. He really wants to learn."

"Yeah, the first time he's out, he nearly wrecks the boat by hitting a rock and throws that girl overboard."

"Travis, aren't you being a little melodramatic? The rafts can take it. I'm sure you've hit plenty of rocks."

"He belongs back on his old man's peanut farm." Travis uttered a few more choice words when he thought she wasn't listening.

Jo sighed and picked up the PFDs to sort them out by sizes. There had to be a way to smooth things over and make Dan accepted among the employees. It wasn't good for company morale to have employees not working together as a team. The customers were sure to notice it, and this business was highly competitive. If other rafting companies knew what was afoot, they would gladly pounce on it. She could already see Chris making the most out of it. *If you want your steak burned, your life in peril, and people at odds with each other, then take a trip with Red Canyon Adventures. But if you want succulent meals and a smooth, friendly trip to see the wonders of nature, then come raft with us.*

Jo wondered what the strategy should be. Talk to the guys about it? Talk to Dan and give him more lessons? She already knew she needed to go on the next overnighter to offer him lessons on camp etiquette. But she knew, too, her reputation was on the line. After all, she was the one who asked Todd to hire the guy. She needed to save herself embarrassment and settle everyone's nerves—a tall order Jo was uncertain she could fill.

Jo finished the work in the storeroom and headed back to the main building. Todd stood at the cash register finishing some paperwork. She lingered at the doorway, observing his movements to see if he was as irritated as Travis. He stood composed, his tanned face smooth, his eyes focused on his work. Todd was usually quite levelheaded. While Travis acted out his frustration, Todd did it undercover. It would not surprise her, for instance, if he'd already fired Dan yet stood there without displaying a hint of emotion.

"So how was your overnighter?" she finally asked him.

"It went great. The customers had a good time."

Hmm. She expected to hear about the steaks burning and Dan keeling over in the sand. "Travis said Dan is having a hard time settling into the routine."

Todd glanced up. "Huh? Not from what I'm seeing. I mean, he didn't cook right the first time, but I remember Travis scorching pancakes on his first cooking duty. Dan did a good job setting up the tents. And the kids love him."

These comments made Jo glow inside. Perhaps she'd not blown it after all in suggesting that Todd hire him. "So you think he's gonna work out with the company?"

Todd shrugged. "Not sure. We're still in the training phase. But he's eager to please and wants this job bad, so that's good. He's not like a certain know-it-all who thinks he has everything figured out when he doesn't." Todd opened the register to take out the day's cash and put it in the safe. "I just wish he'd keep his mouth shut about the way I do things. He's not the head of this place, even if he feels he's earned it."

Uh-oh. Todd and Travis were having issues? They had other employees in the company—Sheryl, Christine, Larry, Chip, Evan—but no one worked more closely together than Todd and Travis. She thought of them like brothers in a way. They often hung out evenings at the tavern, not that she agreed with their habit of having a beer, but they talked business and discussed ways of doing things. Jo wondered if one day Todd might make Travis his business associate. Now to hear they may be butting heads—this was not a good sign.

He went on. "Just the other day he was talking to me about something that Chris was offering at his place. Frankly, I don't care to know what Chris or any of the other competition is doing. I'll run my business the way I want."

Todd was venting, which was probably a good thing. Oftentimes he didn't.

He suddenly backpedaled. "Sorry, I've said too much."

"You need to get it out. Remember what your mom used to say. 'Todd will explode one day if he doesn't get all those things out of him. He just sits there and stews.'"

"Yeah, but it's not good for my employees to hear me talking about them behind their backs. It makes for bad blood. And the customers are going to sense it if we're not a team. So forget I said anything."

Jo could only admire Todd for putting his customers first. And his business, too. No matter what it took. And she was there to make sure it ran smoothly and he was on an even keel with everything. She owed that to their mothers who were as close as sisters could be. They were all close as kids growing up in New York where her parents still lived. Holidays were shared with the entire clan. The cousins hung out and played games or talked until 1:00 a.m. It was only natural that Jo would choose to come out West a few years ago to help Todd with the business when he put out the call. What probably wasn't natural was the true reason she responded to his need for help. Jo had come here to Moab to get away. . . .

She shook her head, not wishing to delve into that memory right now. First thing's first. Make sure her owner-cousin and fellow employees were happy and the business remained afloat. "Todd, you know I'm here to help. If there's anything I can do to make things better, let me know."

"Just be sure you help out where Dan is concerned. I'm having you go along on the next overnighter, too, and teach him how to cook."

"You know, he's really looking forward to skippering his own boat. But I know to be a skipper, you gotta first mop the deck."

Todd gave her a smirk. "And you know he needs to be trained for a solid three weeks. I have no problem with Dan manning a boat after instruction and passing the state test. It will take time, but I think he has what it takes."

Dan would love hearing that. And for some reason, Jo felt eager to give him the good news. Leaving work that night to return to her apartment, she wondered where he lived. Not that she dared go to his apartment, but he talked of renting a nice place and had already bought himself a Jeep. He had the money to settle down. A far cry from when she first came here and had to resort to sleeping on Todd's sofa until she could afford a place of her own. Her vehicle right now was her own two feet or begging off Todd for the use of his car. But there were advantages to living in a town. Her feet did fine, taking her places. Everything was convenient.

Just then she heard a horn toot. A red Jeep pulled up beside her. Dan looked over with a smile parked on his face. "Hey there. Need a lift?"

"Actually, I prefer walking, thanks."

"Okay." She watched in amusement as he attempted to parallel park in a nearby space. After three tries he finally got the Jeep into the space, though cockeyed, and pocketed the keys. "So where are we walking to?"

"Well, I'm walking home."

"Great. I always wanted to know where you live."

Jo didn't say that she wanted to know where he lived, too, but the thought of him discovering her place of residence left her uncomfortable. "Look Dan, I'm not into that kind of thing."

"You mean you're not the kind of girl who invites guys into her apartment. Of course I know that. I mean, Mom lectured me about it long ago. The 'I won't invite myself unless I'm asked' kind of thing. But I can walk there, can't I?"

"I guess so." As they walked, he yammered away about rafting and his first day cooking, leaving out the details about burning the steak. Obviously no one thought it a big deal but Travis. Yet she was curious about his take on what happened. "Travis said you had a problem with the steaks."

"Oh, he got all uptight because I burned one, and I didn't

care to cook a raw one for a customer. Travis had to do it himself. I guess because he guides trips, it's beneath him now to cook. Though I thought everyone was supposed to help out."

"I'm not sure why Travis is acting like this and giving you a hard time."

Dan shrugged. "It's no big deal. So long as the boss isn't upset, that's what counts. I mean, I get along fine with everyone else. Guess Travis gets upset easily over things. Not sure why. Maybe he's wired that way, with a short fuse."

Dan seemed to know a lot about people. The mere thought intrigued her. "Yeah, sometimes people don't react well to difficulties. Though I never thought anything bothered Travis until you came on the scene."

"Maybe we're like oil and water. I mean, Pop once had a fellow farmer he couldn't get along with no matter what he did. The guy insisted that there was only one way to raise peanuts. Pop had other ways of doing things. They even got into a shouting match once about peanuts. I mean, what good does it do? It's probably the same with this guy. He has his way of doing things, and I guess I'm messing up his plan. But he doesn't realize that it makes no sense to get uptight. Life's too short."

"It's good it doesn't bother you."

"Well, not so fast. It does if I let it. Besides, I have you to give me my pills of encouragement each day. Better than a bottle of vitamins." He gave her a huge smile, his face reflecting the setting sun. "I mean, you've been a blessing. Oops."

"What?"

"Now I sound like my mother. She's always saying how this person and that person is a blessing."

"There's nothing wrong with that. It's why God made us, to love Him and to help each other. Love your neighbor as yourself."

For the first time, Dan lapsed into thoughtful stillness. Now another question surfaced in her mind—Dan's faith. Jo's relationship with God meant everything to her. She wondered if it was the same with him. "Your mom must be a strong Christian woman," she said.

"To the T or capital C, I guess. Follows every rule and regulation there is. Hey, you want to stop for a drink? I'm thirsty. Seems I never can get enough to drink out here. It's so dry."

"Yes, it is dry."

She followed him into a café where they sat down and ordered sodas. He consumed his in a few minutes then promptly let out a loud belch. "Oh man, sorry about that."

"That's what happens when you swallow soda quickly." She sipped hers slowly through the straw, even as Dan ordered another one. "So what are you going to do on your day off?"

"Well, I'm hoping you might have the same day off so you can take me on a tour of Moab. I still don't know the half about this town, though I see the Colorado flows nearby on its way south. I kind of wonder why the rafts don't go all the way to town."

"It's too shallow for the boats to make it this far. But Moab is a great little town with its own character. I'll see if Todd can give me the day off; then we can look around." She hesitated. "But I'm not sure. . ."

His smile grew even broader as if she were making his evening complete. She cautioned herself not to become too involved. There were interesting things about Dan, but she should take it slow. She dared not trust her heart to him or lead him on, for that matter. *A simple walk around town would be all right*, she thought, as was having a cola. It didn't send up a smoke signal for a relationship. They were just being friends.

When Dan downed his third cola, he flew to his feet. "Wow, I feel like I can race around the block. With all that caffeine and sugar, I'll be up all night. Then I'll be tired for work tomorrow, and that's not cool." They went outside to find the sun had dipped below the rocky landscape beyond, igniting the area a fiery red. Dan paused to appreciate the scenery. "You never see anything like this in Virginia. It's like something out of an inferno. I can't get over how red the rocks are or the interesting formations. To think that eons of wind and rain did it all."

"You need to visit Arches some day. The national park near here. It has over a hundred natural arch formations inside the park."

They walked along the sidewalk until Jo paused before a kiosk displaying area information. "See?" She pointed to a picture of the famous Delicate Arch, glorified by the sunset.

"I remember seeing that in a magazine back home. That's fantastic."

"Yes, it really is pretty. There's a nice hike to it where you can view it up close." She paused, realizing she was again trying to plan their activities together. She needed to put the brakes on this before she found things careening out of control down the road of life.

"We have a national park in Virginia called Shenandoah. It has a road running the length of the mountains to different overlooks."

"I've been there many times."

He turned to stare at her. "You have? I didn't know that."

Jo paused, realizing her slip. "Well, we traveled a lot," she managed to say.

"We never did. Pop refused to leave his peanuts. And he never trusted anyone else to look after them. But now I don't have to worry about it, because I'm doing the exploring on my own. Seeing all there is to see in life. Everything I've been missing out on. And I'm having a great time, too."

Jo listened to the tone of his voice, almost as if he were challenging his father's rule, though the man was a thousand miles away. What happened in Virginia to send Dan here? She would love to explore it more, but again she didn't want to open her heart further. As it was, she'd probably said too much already.

"Well, this is where we part ways. My place is over there."

He stood still, his hands in his pockets. Thankfully he kept them there and made no move to take her hand or anything else. They stood on the sidewalk in the fading sunset, looking into each other's eyes. This was getting more uncomfortable by the second. Jo looked to a small gift shop across the street. "Guess I'll see you in the morning, bright and early."

"Yep. I'm with an early morning group. Same river trip. I think Todd will let me do the boat again, and this time, no rocks."

"You'll do fine." She saw him take his hands out of his pockets. He took a step forward. *Uh-oh. He's on the move.* She gave a brief smile, turned, and walked away. He didn't follow. She hastened for her apartment and when she arrived, closed the door behind her and breathed a sigh of relief. *What are you doing, Jo? Why are you letting this guy into your life? Taking you out for a soda? Talking to him? And then of all things, you offer to spend your day off with him!*

She sighed and opened her laptop to access Facebook.

She typed onto her wall—*I refuse to open up my heart until the timing is right*. She then saw a friend request from Dan Mallory. She went to his page to see his smiling face. The background scenery of the photo appeared like the kind found back East. There were no red rocks or bright sun, just lots of green. She missed the greenery of the eastern forests and farmlands. Lush trees and tall grasses. An abundance of flowers in springtime, like the colorful mixture of dogwood, redbud, and azaleas. She hit the key to accept his request. It shouldn't change the status of their relationship if they were simply friends on a computer.

She looked around at various pages until suddenly the chat box popped up. Dan had logged on.

AHA. THOUGHT YOU MIGHT BE ONLINE. THANKS FOR ACCEPTING MY FRIEND REQUEST.

Jo pondered how to answer. WELL, ONE FRIEND'S AS GOOD AS ANOTHER, she typed.

YES, BUT WE HAVE A UNIQUE FRIENDSHIP. WE ARE FRIENDS OF THAT GREAT RIVER KNOWN AS THE COLORADO. AND THOSE FRIENDS MUST STAY TOGETHER AND SEE WHERE IT LEADS THEM OR DROWN.

Jo considered that one. ARE YOU DROWNING?

NO WAY. I'M ALIVE AND I'M AFLOAT, THANKS TO YOU.

Jo felt warmth rush into her cheeks and decided she'd better end this session quickly. WELL, I'M PRETTY TIRED. ANOTHER BIG DAY TOMORROW.

OKAY, NIGHT NOW. SWEET DREAMS.

Even at home she couldn't seem to get away from the man. Closing the laptop, she realized she needed to cool this off somehow. Give him the proverbial cold shoulder. Claim she was too busy for get-togethers. Though she was the one who agreed to a tour of Moab on a mutual day off. She sighed.

God, I know You brought Dan here for a reason. I'm not sure what to make of it all. But until I know his heart and where he stands with You, Lord, I pray that somehow You keep us separated. Please don't let me lose my heart over this or be tempted. Provide me a way out. I want my heart to belong to You and You alone until the time is right for a man to enter my life. In Jesus' name.

She felt better after the prayer but still wondered in the days ahead how she would relate to Dan. She would still be seeing him day after day. There was that camping trip together coming up. A day off sometime in the future to explore Moab. Maybe even a hiking trip to Delicate Arch. None of this lined up with the prayer she'd just offered. Well, God would have to change the plans. Or change Dan's interest. Or do something wild and crazy. Or maybe she needed to do the changing. Take charge of her life and her destiny. Let Dan know that being pals on a social network was fine, but that was all. At least for now.

five

Booyah! Dan, you're the man. He was feeling good today, and not just because the sun was shining as it always did. Or the blue skies loomed above without a hint of clouds. Or there was another round of hot, dry weather as was typical. He was just glad to be here, doing what he could only dream of doing a few months ago. Sure, there had been a few hiccups along the way and the steely-eyed look of Travis whenever something minutely went wrong. But Todd liked what he did. Everyone else was friendly. And plans for a relationship with Jo were coming along nicely, with online chats and the one afternoon when they toured the sites of Moab. Sometimes Dan wished their relationship would take off on a swift jog or even a fast run. But Jo was not that kind of girl. He could read between the lines. She had principles. For instance, she never wore anything out of line. Her clothing was conservative—mainly hiking apparel. She wore little make-up and tiny hoop earrings. She was perfectly tanned, nicely proportioned, and had fabulous legs. She was also careful with online social network places. They'd chatted a few times about nothing personal but everything friendly.

Dan knew, though, that something must be happening between them, because everyone else seemed to sense it. He realized it the day he stumbled into the office to find Travis there with a friend of his. Usually the boss didn't approve of outside friends moseying around the place, but Travis ignored the policy and brought his friend in anyway to help himself to the donuts and coffee. It was then that Dan overheard Travis complaining about him, intermixed with whispers about Jo.

"Yeah, you can tell Dan and Jo are already starting something. And of course, whenever something good is coming Jo's way, Todd wants to make sure it works out. Guess he thinks Jo deserves a guy in her life after coming here to help him."

That didn't sound too bad to Dan, until Travis began pointing out Dan's faults. And how Jo had to come on the next overnight trip to babysit him. "Isn't that just cozy."

Though Dan did like the idea of Jo being by his side, he didn't appreciate Travis gossiping to his friend and patronizing him. So Dan strode into the office with what he hoped was a cheesy "gotcha" smile on his face and asked what they were talking about. Travis stood his ground, but the friend looked away. Dan continued to make small talk while pouring some fresh brew and then walked out whistling a jingle.

Now Dan was looking forward to the overnight trip planned for this weekend. They had a decent group reserved—three families each complete with mom, pop, and kids. The best part of all was that Jo would help him smooth out the kinks in the cooking arena, though Dan knew perfectly well how to cook. The burned steak had been a fluke. Could've happened to anyone. But if it opened the door for Jo and him to interact, he'd take it.

Just then he heard a greeting and whirled to find Jo entering the building. She looked great to him even if she wore hiking shorts, a T-shirt, and had her hair pulled back by an elastic band. "C'mon Dan, we've got shopping to do."

One day we're gonna go shopping for that diamond. . . . He halted. Where did *that* come from? He'd only known her a few weeks. Marriage was a huge step. He could see it a year from now, arriving back at the farm with Jo in tow and the looks of astonishment on Pop and Mom's faces when he announced, "Hey folks, meet the wife!"

"Dan, are you listening to me?"

"Sure, I like to shop, depending on what it is. What are we shopping for?"

"We need to get the rest of the food for the trip. Normally Todd does it, but he asked us to go so he could check on a raft that we need for this trip. Somehow it isn't inflating properly."

"Is that bad to be one short?"

"It is when you're fully booked like we are this weekend. So I hope we can get it fixed, or we're gonna have to rent one somewhere."

She slung her backpack purse over her shoulders. It certainly wasn't like the huge bag his mom carried. He liked it. "Nice bag."

Jo looked at him in surprise and wrinkled her face. "What? You mean my purse?"

"Yeah, it's not huge. Just right for an outdoorsy girl like you."

"What do you know about a woman's purse?"

"Nothing, except the one I see my mom lugging around. She has one you could fit car parts into."

Jo laughed. "I like this one 'cause it's more like a day pack than a purse. Sometimes people frown on carrying a day pack into stores."

"When I went to DC for a trip a few years back, you couldn't carry anything bigger than a camera case into public buildings." His voice faded. Another memory surfaced, of a family trip to Washington DC to celebrate Pop's birthday.

It was one of the few times they managed to lure Pop away from the peanut field for a family outing. He wanted to see the Air and Space Museum. They had a great time exploring the Apollo spacecraft, the airplanes, and the cases of moon rocks. And of course, watching the IMAX film. For a moment he was transported to that time, and the laughter of his family in his ears was real.

"Dan? Hello? Are you alive?"

Jo's concern brought him back to reality. "Just thinking." He didn't elaborate on his thoughts. If he did, she was sure to ask questions about family stuff, maybe even tell him he needed to go back home and straighten things out. That he shouldn't have upped and left his family like he did with no one to take his place. "But I have a life, too," he argued. "And I plan to live it."

"Dan, you'd better tell me what this is all about."

"Sorry. I was thinking aloud. It has nothing to do with you, I promise." He smiled, and she smiled back. All was forgiven and hopefully forgotten.

They walked down the road to the grocery store where Jo suggested they each grab carts. His cart was soon filled with fresh vegetables and meats, hers with snacks, soft drinks, and desserts. "This looks like enough to feed the first battalion," he commented.

"Everyone always gets hungry when they're out on these trips. They'll eat you clean. But that's okay. They're paying for it."

Dan nearly flipped over the amount Jo forked over at the cash register. Several hundred bucks gone. But it would certainly make for happy campers when the adults saw the steaks, and the kids the Kool-Aid and cookies.

Jo wheeled the cart loaded down with bags until she

suddenly stopped. "I don't believe how dumb I am."

"What? You're not dumb."

She threw up her hands. "How are we going to get this stuff back to the shop? I forgot to borrow Todd's SUV."

Dan should have thought of that, too, though he had been slightly distracted. But now he could be the hero and rescue a damsel loaded down with two dozen shopping bags. "No problem. I'll go get my Jeep. It's not that many blocks away."

"Thanks. And can you hurry? We have pricey perishables. I'll go back inside and keep this stuff in air-conditioning."

"Be right back."

Dan wasted no time jogging down the street toward the rafting center. He dodged in and around shoppers cruising the town, young couples holding hands, and older citizens gawking at the postcards and trinkets in souvenir shops that said Moab in a dozen different ways. All signs of a thriving tourist town and a place he was glad to be a part of. He arrived and climbed into his Jeep, returning to the store where Jo stood waiting by some soda machines.

"I'm sorry about this."

"What are you sorry for?" He hauled bag after bag, loading each into the back end of the Jeep until it was full.

"Sorry that I'm not thinking. I hope I can get my act together before the trip. I'm supposed to be the trainer, and you're the trainee."

"I think it's good if people can help each other out of situations. Can't get much better training than that. Two are better than one anyway."

Jo turned quiet. He started the engine, hoping he didn't scare her with the hint of some diamond solitaire in the future with the "two are better than one" comment. It just seemed the right thing to say.

"I know you're right," Jo finally answered. He perked up at her agreement. Maybe he wasn't so off track with the relationship angle after all.

Having placed the meat and veggies into the large refrigerator unit and packing the rest into dry bags, he and Jo then began sorting out camping gear. They packed tents, cots, and sleeping bags for everyone, along with other gear like lanterns, tableware, and cooking supplies. "There's a lot to think about with this kind of trip," he mused.

"Normally we have a checklist, but I know the routine by heart. Still, I should show it to you." She left and soon returned with a clipboard holding multiple pages. "See what I mean?"

"This is good for someone like me who's always disorganized." He scanned it carefully. "Looks like we've covered all the basics."

Jo laughed. "You'd better read the list and make sure we haven't forgotten anything. I don't think Mr. and Mrs. Harris would like it if we have the tent but no cots for them to sleep on."

"But sleeping on nice, soft sand isn't so bad."

"No, it's not." She paused. He saw a red flush enter her cheeks that could not be from the wind and sun. Again he wondered if he'd said the wrong thing, but he was just making a camping comment. He liked cowboy camping in the great outdoors on the soft ground. He and Rob used to do stuff like that when they were young. Wander into the woods, pick out a nice spot, and bed down for the night. He went ahead and told her about it to ease her discomfort.

"Oh sure, I totally agree with you. I don't know, I guess I feel weird talking about that kind of stuff with you."

Now it was Dan's turn to feel a flush creep into his face. "I don't understand."

"Never mind." She took off in the direction of the office. He dearly wanted to follow, to press the issue and find out what was going on underneath that gorgeous mound of thick brown hair caught up in a hair band. Maybe this meant she did have feelings for him. Maybe she thought about him. Admired his physique and his winning personality. At least he was tanning up nicely after the initial sunburn, along with sporting a lean build, nifty sunglasses, and of course, the fantastic red Jeep. If all that couldn't land him a girl, what would?

His heart began to pound in anticipation. He had no worries. They were going together on a camping trip to help the customers but also to work as a team. And when the customers drifted off to sleep, there was the moonlight creating that shimmering effect on the river and Jo sitting beside him, taking it all in. What a perfect opportunity for a kiss and a cuddle. *Take it easy, Dan the man. One step at a time.*

❧

The rafting part of the trip went well, with the kids and their parents loving every minute. They screamed and cheered and laughed all the way down the rapids. They were modest rapids according to Todd, good enough for little guys and girls who found small bounces in the boat a great thrill. For his part, Dan was mesmerized by Jo who sat in the other boat. The wind tousled her hair, and the loosened strands floated in the breeze. Her face broke out in smiles. One time she raised her hand as if she were waving at him. He waved back, and she turned away to focus on her paddle. It didn't matter. She was still amazing to look at. He couldn't wait for the camping part of the trip when they would work together.

The spot Todd chose for camping was an area utilized by other rafting companies—a large stretch of sandy beach surrounded by red rocks and cliffs, and flanked by the gentle flow of the river. Here the kids could play around with their parents—building sand castles or wading in the river while he and the crew readied the camp. Dan wanted Jo to help him erect the tents, but she was setting up the camp kitchen. He didn't worry. They would be working together soon enough.

"You're the first guy I've ever hired that knew about tents right off, Dan," Todd commented. "You're a natural at this."

"Virginia is for campers. Lots of places to camp with the mountains and all."

Todd laughed. "Must be why Jo knew about it, too, having lived there for a while. Guess with the mountains, there's plenty of recreation."

Dan was suddenly caught up in the first part of Todd's statement. *Jo is also from Virginia?* Where? Why didn't she mention it? What was her reason for coming here?

He turned and saw Jo waving at him, and this time she meant it. "C'mon, Dan. I need you to help make the salad."

He walked over. "Did you say make the salad? But I'd rather cook the steaks. Isn't salad making the woman's job?"

She cast him an evil eye. "Don't start with me now. Here's the tomatoes. Go ahead and cut them up."

Dan tried to hide his displeasure as Jo worked on getting the other parts of the meal ready. "Todd says you're from Virginia."

She gave him a look he couldn't decipher while she held bags of dinner rolls in each hand. "So what?"

"Well, I am, too. You knew that, didn't you?"

She shrugged.

"C'mon. Isn't that interesting that we're both from the same state? Where did you live? Why did you come out here? Don't you find it a lot different than Virginia?"

"A man of a thousand questions. Yes, I did live in Virginia for a time, near Leesburg. And of course, Utah is different from Virginia."

She answered the questions but left out all the juicy details that women usually loved to provide. In the meantime, he just missed chopping off the tip of his finger. "So you're not going to elaborate."

"There isn't much else to say. I came out here to help Todd. And because things weren't working out too great with my brother in Virginia."

Ah. . .some description at last as he watched Jo set out the steaks on a board and season them. Again he wished she was here at the cutting board dicing tomatoes and he was manning the grill. He felt like a housewife.

"You really have an ego problem," she suddenly remarked.

His chopping abruptly halted. "Me?"

"Yes. I can see it in your face. Don't worry. You're gonna cook the steaks like a barbecue maestro. I understand these guy things, being around my brother and Todd."

He chuckled. "Jo, you can read me like a book. Do you also know that. . ." He paused. It almost came rattling out of him. *Do you also know that I think you're something else? More than something else? That I would like to date you and maybe kiss you and see where the future leads us. . . .*

"C'mon, let's get the steaks on the grill."

He reluctantly abandoned his attraction for Jo, which shouldn't be rearing its head right now, anyway, since the moon hadn't yet risen. He went over to the grill. Charcoal smoke smarted his eyes but made his mouth water at the same time. He stood by the steaks, turning them every so often. As they cooked, the guests wandered by, taking in the deep aroma of the food while enjoying the summer evening. Dan heard a variety of remarks, everything from how yummy the steaks looked to "I hope you didn't forget that I asked for tofu burgers." Jo had those tucked away in the cooler.

"You're doing a great job, Dan," Jo observed. She stood fairly close to him now, and though her eyes were focused on the steaks, his gaze was focused on the top of her head. He could see the long part down the middle of her hair, the way she often wore it. He wondered what her hair smelled like—probably a combination of the great outdoors and charcoal.

When the meal was cooked and the guests served, it was time for the staff to eat. Jo cooked the rest of the steaks and tofu burgers for them. Dan was all set to help himself to the remaining steak when Travis came along and snatched up the last hunk. "Sorry," he said with a grin.

Dan shrugged and looked at the three tofu burgers staring back at him. He could have a tofu burger. Combining it with lettuce and onions, drowned in ketchup, it would be just fine and healthier, too. *You ain't gonna win either, Travis.* He sat companionably with everyone else, watching Jo from where she sat opposite him, indulging in her nice piece of steak and salad that he'd fixed. They talked about the trip thus far, the pancake breakfast the next morning, and who would be leading the night stalk with the kids after dark.

"I nominate Dan to do the night stalk," Travis announced.

"Dan cooked tonight," declared Jo. "Why don't you do it, Travis?"

"I don't mind," Dan said. "I like doing the night stalk. As a kid, we did one with our flashlights in a campground with a ranger, near the Blue Ridge Parkway. Someone saw a bear. That was the quickest stalking we ever did."

Everyone laughed long and loud, including Jo. Everyone, that is, but Travis. Dan laughed, too, in spite of himself. He was quickly nominated night stalk captain of the evening.

When they began cleaning up, Jo sauntered up to him, her face beaming. "Dan, you are nothing short of the man tonight."

"I am?" He tried to hide his pleasure behind a straight face, but it was tough. A small smile managed to seep out.

"Sure. I mean having a good attitude about things, even if you didn't like making the salad. And volunteering to do the night stalk. You're pretty amazing."

Thank You, God. I'm in heaven. And he meant it. Not that he talked much to God these days, but maybe he ought to. God was blessing him big-time, and Jo was getting more and more intriguing. Especially when she announced that she wanted to tag along on the night stalk with the kiddos. *We're a team, God; we're a team.*

And a team they were, leading the kids along the riverbank by flashlight where they found creatures that came out at night—different kinds of bugs and lizards, and they even heard the howl of a coyote on a distant cliff. As they headed back for the yellow glow reflecting in the propane lanterns that lit up the campsite, Jo walked beside him, her flashlight shining this way and that. "Well, this has been a great day, Dan."

"It sure has." And it was only just the beginning. The night was still young.

"You know, when I came here from Virginia, I wondered if I'd ever have days like this. I mean, I came here not only to help Todd but hoping for a change in my life. And then I found out life is pretty much the same wherever you go."

"No way."

"Huh?"

"It's been great for me so far. This is where I needed to be. Do you think I had this much fun raising peanuts? No way."

"But stuff still follows you. The discontent that brought you here. It doesn't matter how far you travel either. You may not see it right now. It took me awhile to see that life was not any different than back home. There were still troubles and trials and my own problems to work out. I'm just glad I know God. He's helped me so much in many areas."

Dan began kicking up sand as he walked. "You sound like Mom and Pop."

"What do you mean?"

"They talk like God is some kind of buddy in the sky waiting to offer a lift on His go-cart. I'm not sure how anyone can see God like that."

"I'd hardly call God a buddy, but He is a friend in times of need. And above all, He is Lord of my life."

Dan nearly tripped over a stick. He caught himself in time and then stopped, even as the kids raced over to be reunited with their parents and share in the marshmallow roast now in full progress. God was Lord of her life? No longer just a friend but also some great King on a fancy throne, giving out dos and don'ts? How could He be both? What did this really mean?

When they heard Todd asking them to hand out the makings for s'mores, Jo left him to pitch in with the work. Dan could only stand and watch her place a child's well-charred marshmallow between chunks of chocolate and graham crackers. She handed it back to the wide-eyed, eager kid.

God is Lord of Jo's life? *And* God is a friend? He realized then he didn't know God at all. Maybe in name only, but that's it. And maybe he didn't know Jo that well either. If a pin could burst a balloon, it just did with several simple yet profound words. *He is Lord of my life.*

six

What Jo said that evening at the campsite stuck like one of those burrs, not in Dan's sock but in his brain. Though he tried hard not to think about it, the message continued to remain in his thoughts. She was just like his folks when it came to things of God. If there was one thing he wanted to do, it was to escape all the religiosity. He certainly didn't want Jo to know this, however, as it was obvious God meant a great deal to her. That was okay by him, so long as he didn't have to believe it, too. Or maybe he could give the semblance of being part of the religious gang. Like saying the proverbial "Well, praise God!" when something good happened, or bowing his head in dutiful prayer when it came to thanking the Lord for his food. All the things he'd grown up with back at the farm.

At times though, Dan felt like he owed God a great deal more than platitudes. God did see fit to give him a fantastic job here in Moab. Dan had a great apartment with a huge bedroom. The main living room held the forty-two-inch HDTV and the Xbox. He had his red Jeep to cruise around town. Nice Oakley shades to wear. Everything a man could want, save a girlfriend clinging to his arm, which he hoped to remedy soon.

Jo did like the way the camping trip turned out, so Dan felt he was making strides in the area of a relationship. He knew when she was surfing the Internet and managed to snag her for a few impromptu chats. They saw each other quite a bit on the business front, even though the rafting trips kept him busy most days. They hadn't gone out to eat in a while, but Dan knew he also couldn't appear overly eager by asking for dates and risk sending her in the opposite direction. He had to take this all step-by-step. Except for the God part. The Lord of her life part. That he had a hard time reconciling.

Dan arrived home after a day on the river, overheated as usual and looking for a drink to quench his thirst. Despite the copious amounts of suntan lotion, he still felt like a chicken cooking in the hot Utah sun. The sun was relentless in this place, shining day in and day out. He had seen one afternoon thunderstorm since his arrival. No wonder the ground was baked to hard clay. The red rocks kept the heat, too, reflecting the intensity of it at night, long after the sun went down. But it was still a neat place, even if it felt like an oven. And he never stopped marveling at the rock formations they passed by each day on the rafting trips. He knew them all by heart and liked pointing out things like the Gummy Bear formation to the thrill of the kids. He was at ease explaining to the guests the various geological features and even the version of how old the formations were—made a zillion years ago from the big bang or something like that, though it went against everything Pop taught him about creation. He also liked the water antics they played on the raft—the tug-o'-war games, sneaking up on other rafts for water fights, and taking a dive backward out of the raft to the delight of the passengers.

Dan now relaxed on the sofa of his apartment, sipping a cold drink, feeling a bit drowsy. The air-conditioning felt good. He was ready to drift off to happy land when his cell phone played a rock-and-roll tune.

"Hey-lo," he answered, his eyes still closed.

"Hi, Dan."

A sweet feminine voice filled his ear. Instantly he was awake, as was every nerve in his body. "Hi, Jo. Wassup?"

"Not much. I just closed down the store and. . ."

"Great, you wanna get a bite to eat?" He cringed, realizing how swiftly the invitation came streaming out of him.

"No, not that. The reason I'm calling is that Travis says you lost some gear today."

"Huh?" His hand squeezed the tiny phone he held. "What's he talking about? I checked in all the gear from my boat."

"The numbers aren't adding up. We're short on PFDs and two sets of paddles."

"Well, see if it's from his boat." He tried not to let the words come out in a snarl.

"Dan, I don't know whose boat they're from. I'm just telling you what he told me."

"Yeah." He was ready to let it all out—what he truly thought of Travis. "I'll be right there." He stood to his feet, his muscles stiff from being in near-sleep mode. He felt a strange twitch in his neck, probably from the day's paddling. Todd told him that soon he might be ready to tackle some of the more adventurous parts of the river. Dan wasn't sure he'd ever be ready for a place like Cataract Canyon. But maybe if it got him away from Travis, he would take Todd up on it.

He put on his baseball cap and grabbed his car keys, wallet, and drink bottle. Well, maybe all things were working out for good. If he went over there and straightened this out, then maybe Jo would feel better about going out to eat with him. He wouldn't appear to be playing the guy chasing after the girl scenario. He could make it one of those buddy-type meetings to discuss work, maybe even ask her about the Cataract Canyon rafting trips as a cover. That sounded like a good plan.

The Jeep was steaming hot to the touch, thanks to the one-hundred-degree heat that had not dissipated despite it being 7:00 p.m. It didn't take him long to drive over and head directly to the building where the equipment was stored. Jo stood there along with Todd, trying to sort it all out. "I turned in all my stuff," he announced to Todd.

"Well, we're off on the count. You checked in each of the PFDs?"

"Yes, along with the paddles."

Todd scratched his head. "It's not adding up. And I don't like being short. We have a sold-out excursion tomorrow. I have to find the missing gear."

"We must have more life jackets lying around," Jo said. "The paddles could be in a different area."

"I don't like this when I have a mega group coming the next day. They're a business group, too. I wanted everything ready to go. This stinks."

Dan was unsure what to say or do. He did recall at the river earlier that day, when they had stopped for a break, that Travis appeared tense. And some of the people on his raft were not wearing life jackets.

"Dan, is something up?" Jo asked.

He blinked, wondering how she would know. Did his face have neon words filtering across it? Could she read what was in his mind? She couldn't possibly know his ulterior motive—that his coming here and showing interest was actually a cover-up for a planned dinner date later tonight. "Uh. . .only that a couple of Travis's passengers didn't have PFDs on when we left the beach area. I noticed it when we were already on the river, but I thought the guests had taken them off for some reason."

Todd stared. "What? But that's against company policy. Are you sure?"

"Yeah, but I know he'll deny it. He's been after me ever since I started this job."

"I wonder why Travis would do that," Jo said. "It doesn't sound like him."

"No, but I'm about to get to the bottom of this," Todd said.

Todd strode away while Dan watched in apprehension. If Todd opened his mouth that he'd blabbed about Travis, it could land him in hot water. "Hey Jo, I don't want him telling Travis that I said anything." He swiped his hands together in agitation.

"He won't."

Dan wasn't so sure. He thought again about Jo's words. *God is the Lord of my life.* If He is Lord, then He is in control. And He could handle people like Travis and his jealousy, keeping dear old Dan out of boiling water and from getting beat up by the bullies of Moab. Right?

"Dan, it will be okay." Again came Jo's soothing voice, so much like nice cold ice cream easing his dry throat.

He swallowed to find his throat raw like sandpaper. He badly needed a cold drink. He headed over to the back door that led to the store and helped himself to a drink out of the case. He then checked it off on the employee list posted by the cash register. Jo followed him and now stood in the doorway. The fading red hues of sun framed her like a fiery halo effect. She looked stunning to him. And mysterious. And ready to pronounce once more—*God is the Lord of my life.* And he, Dan, might have to bow down right there.

"You really are bothered by this."

He finished the drink in several long swallows. "Travis and I have never gotten along. Maybe he thinks I'm here to take over the roost. All I wanted was a fun job on the river. But he doesn't like how I handle the customers. What I do with the kids. How

I cook. How I pack the gear in the boats. And he says I don't give correct safety instructions. Like what is there to give? Stay in the boat and love your guide stuff, mostly."

"Well, he certainly can't talk about safety if he's allowing passengers to ride without wearing the proper safety equipment. If Todd finds out its true, he'll can him."

Dan stared. "You mean he'll fire Travis?"

"It's a violation, and if one of those passengers fell overboard and drowned, do you know what would happen to us? A lawsuit, maybe even charges of negligence."

Dan never thought about that. He then remembered the first time he manned a craft and the girl with the earrings who fell overboard while trying to retrieve her shiny jewelry from the Colorado. It never dawned on him the other aspects of this job, like safety and people getting hurt and lawsuits. He was glad then he didn't hold the reins of control over this operation. He was only a measly employee thankful for a job.

Todd finally arrived back, his face redder than it had been when he left. "Travis insists his people were all wearing their PFDs. He says it was you that didn't have them on your people, Dan."

Dan stood there, feeling as if one of those orange water coolers filled with ice were dumped on him. He felt a chill. There were actual goose bumps breaking out on his tanned forearms. He could barely choke out the words, "But that's not true." He looked to Jo for help. "I did everything by the book, boss. I will swear on. . ." He hesitated until he saw Jo's brown eyes soften. ". . .on a stack of Bibles. I mean, the Lord knows it and everything. I wouldn't do something like that. I know the rules, and I care about people's safety."

Todd's hands flew in the air. "So who am I supposed to believe? It's your word against his. And frankly, Dan, you're the new kid on the block. If I had to go on my gut reaction, I'd say it's the new one on board who may have overlooked a safety measure."

Oh, no. Would he be walking the streets of Moab with a GIVE ME A JOB, PLEASE! sign dangling from his neck? He thought fast and furiously. The group he handled today was all one family. The parents and four kiddos. And he recalled the mom and dad saying they were staying at a certain RV park outside of town. "I'll do what I need to do to clear my name then," Dan said stoutly. "I know where the family is staying that I helped guide today. I'll go right now and ask them if they all had on life jackets and if they will swear by it."

Jo stared at him, as did Todd. "Todd, don't you see? If Dan is willing to go find the family to clear his name, then it's obvious who the guilty party is. And I don't know why Travis won't admit it."

"And I'm willing to prove it," Dan declared. "Anything so I won't get canned."

Todd's eyebrow rose. "Nobody's talking about canning you, Dan. You're a great worker." He began to pace. "I'll talk to Travis again and try to find out what happened. But if you want to get a statement from the family, go for it. It will give me proof with Travis, too, and make things a whole lot easier."

Dan was more than happy to oblige. Anything to clear up this matter once and for all. He immediately headed for his Jeep and jumped in. Only then did he see Jo standing nearby, watching him. "You can come along if you want. Probably should, as I have no idea where this RV park is located."

"How will you find the family?" she asked, entering the passenger seat. "I mean, there's a ton of campers this time of year. It will take a miracle."

"Well, you believe in them, don't you? I'm sure you do. Quoting God and all."

"Of course I do. Every day is a miracle. Don't you think so?"

"I hope there's one for me today. So start praying for a miracle, my dear."

And that's just what she did. She prayed as if God were actually sitting in the backseat of Dan's red Jeep, listening, nodding His great head, or whatever kind of head God possessed, ready to act on his behalf. Dan was at a loss for words when she finished and sat back with a slight smile on her face. She looked as if she enjoyed the one-way conversation. Or maybe it was two-way—though Dan admitted he was hard of hearing these days.

Heading north out of town, they arrived at the Red Rocks RV Park mentioned by the father of the family. At least Dan had the name of the family from the roster. He went to the campground office and checked in with the owner. A grizzly man looked at him over the tops of his reading glasses and shook his head. "Look, I don't know who you are from Adam. I'm not going to tell you where those people are camped."

Dan always wondered why older people compared a person to Adam. He tried to stay calm, but the agitation within was clearly building. His job was on the line. His integrity. And the need to nail Travis and prove him a liar.

"Sir, this is an important safety issue we're dealing with in our rafting company," Jo intervened. "We're hoping to find out about some missing life jackets and paddles. And we need to know if the family accidentally kept them in their possession or if they know where they might be."

"Guess you don't do good inventory at your company then," he said with a huff.

The door creaked open just then and two girls walked into

the store. "Hey, look, it's Raft Man!"

Dan whirled. The kids on the trip had christened him by that name. Sure enough, he recognized the two girls that had been on the raft that day. "Hey there!" he managed to say.

"Hey, Raft Man. We had a great time today. We're just here to buy ice cream."

Dan saw the startled look on the manager's face that matched the disbelief in his heart. "Hey, I was wondering if your dad is around. I gotta ask him something about the trip today."

The girls grabbed his hand. "C'mon, our campsite isn't too far away."

Dan looked over at Jo with a grin. She came alongside as the girls chatted away about the trip.

"Did you find the life jacket okay to wear?" Jo asked.

"No, but Raft Man made us wear them. Though I'm a good swimmer. See, here's our camper. Dad cooked hot dogs for dinner."

Dan went over, introduced himself, and promptly told the man what had happened. In no time the man had written on a piece of paper confirming that his family wore life jackets the entire trip and had turned them in, along with their paddles. "I wouldn't even think of letting my kids go without," he said. "Or my wife and me, for that matter. Why, is there a problem?"

"Just a personal matter we need to clear up about equipment check-in," Jo said with smile. "But we appreciate you taking the time to help us."

"Well, have a hot dog. I've got plenty left. The kids had a great time out there today. Glad we chose your company. There's so many. We just happened to stumble on it while walking in town."

Dan munched down his hot dog while thanking the man

between bites. When he and Jo headed back for the Jeep, his thoughts swirled from the entire scene.

"There," Jo pronounced with a smile.

"There what?"

"You got your miracle. Now do you believe?"

"Yeah, it was definitely a miracle. I mean here we were, asking that manager about the family. He's looking at us and saying there's no way he's gonna tell us anything. Then presto, in walk the two girls from the trip. Pretty amazing stuff."

"There," she pronounced again. "Now do you see why He is Lord of my life? I mean, who else could have orchestrated things so perfectly? You could not have planned it better if you tried. God knew where we were going. He knew the girls would want to buy ice cream. He knew we would meet them and you would get the information you needed to save your job. Dan, God cares about you."

Another proverbial statement often spoken to him in his younger days. But coming from Jo and on the heels of what they had just witnessed at the campground, there was truth behind it. God cared. Why He did. . .Dan didn't know. He never gave God a reason to care. He'd left Him behind for Utah, along with everything else. The thought suddenly made him uncomfortable.

At least he did end up with a date night of sorts with Jo, even if it was eating a hot dog together and seeing a miracle take place at an RV park. His job was spared, his reputation intact. And he had Jo to thank, in part, for it. But one thing was for certain. He had to get Jo completely on his side. Not just the friendly side of things or the religious side of things either, but the serious side. The relationship side. And he thought he knew just how to do it.

seven

Jo loved her days off. She could sleep in and read the Bible or a good novel while lounging in bed. Turn on the laptop and tweet or look at Facebook. Make cinnamon swirl coffee and lounge around in sleepwear until noon. Glance out the window to see the air rippling from the heat and watch people sweating as they went about their daily duties. Sit back and whisper thanks for sweet air-conditioning. Doze in the recliner. Check the clock and see if there's time to munch before polishing off a bag of reduced-fat Oreos.

Jo had elected to indulge in the lounging part so far today, a mug of java in her hands, when the doorbell sounded. She tensed. That could only mean one thing, and as far as she knew, he was working today. *Thank goodness*, she told herself. As much as she liked hanging around with Dan, he was starting to dampen her spiritual nerves. He had a capability of wheedling his way into her life while trying not to look like it. She probably shouldn't be reading into their innocent activities of late, but she had a distinct impression that he was attracted to her. And that wasn't a good thing at this stage of the game.

Jo glanced through the security hole to see the deliveryman with his magic clipboard. She cracked open the door in curiosity to see a large box resting at the man's feet. "I didn't order anything."

"Jolene Davidson?"

"Yes, but. . ."

"Sign here." He thrust the electronic board at her.

Who shipped me this huge box? she wondered as she signed her name. She then saw the logo of an outdoor shop on it. Okay, someone had stolen her ID and was now sending her weird stuff via her credit card. She considered refusing it, but the deliveryman had disappeared, leaving her with the box.

Might as well see what it is, she mused. She carefully zipped open the box with a small paring knife. Inside a plastic bag rested a brand-new backpack. "What?" She rummaged inside the box for the shipping information. The form clearly had her name on it, along with the purchaser's name. Daniel J. Mallory.

"Dan, this isn't going to change things one bit," she mumbled, even as her curiosity got the better of her. She lifted out the backpack to find a newfangled lightweight model with plenty of outside pockets, a padded hip belt, and a place for a hydration system. It certainly was nice—and expensive, too. "I can't accept this, God," she said aloud. Oh, how a part of her wanted to. She always wanted a nice backpack, especially with the camping trips on the river. A place to store her stuff. And then opportunities for backpacking into the wilds of Arches or even Canyonlands. But not from a man she really should be avoiding. If anything, this ought to be raising the red warning flag that the hurricane winds were starting to blow, and she'd better take cover fast.

With reluctance, Jo placed the backpack in its plastic bag and back into the box. She didn't relish the idea of having to pay shipping to send it back, but she couldn't keep it either. *But maybe if I did keep it, use it for a good purpose, tell Dan that it means nothing, but if he wants to spend his money so foolishly. . .*

Quit it, Jo. You can't accept this. It amounts to accepting a relationship. And you're not the dating type. You're the wait-on-God type.

So much for a day off to lounge around and relax. Now her nerves were standing on edge. The package, combined with two cups of coffee, multiplied it. Her stomach began to churn. She made herself a piece of toast spread thick with strawberry jam and sat watching the people on the street. Neighbors were doing their daily routine. A few dog walkers were out and about, intermixed with tourists holding digital cameras. On a distant horizon loomed the fiery splendor that made up the national park nestled beside Moab. Maybe she should take advantage of the day and spend some time in Arches National Park. Pack up an early dinner and go for an evening hike to watch the sun set behind the park's most famous natural feature, Delicate Arch. Get back in tune with God's purposes for her life rather than tuning into Dan's actions, like sending her the backpack. She needed God's tuning, certainly. His voice speaking to her spirit and directing her path.

Some of this is my fault, also, she admitted. *I was too friendly with Dan in the beginning.* He seemed so eager to please. Todd did like him a great deal. Despite the friction with Travis, Dan was working out with the company. He liked kids, too, which was a bonus. He loved a good outdoor adventure—another plus. But he would have nothing to do with God—a huge minus that erased all the plusses. She refused to shirk, either, when it came to telling Dan about her Christian beliefs. She wanted to wear it like an ad on her shirt in the hopes that something might rub off on him.

But now she looked at the big box. So much for conviction. The only thing he was being convicted of was the idea that they were a couple. Phooey on that.

Her cell phone played *Amazing Grace*. It was Dan calling in. She ignored it. Then it signaled an incoming text message. She couldn't resist checking it.

DID YOU GET THE SURPRISE?

Jo stared at the words. Yeah, some surprise. Why didn't you just send a big note with it that said, *I've got the hots for you. Will you be mine?* She chewed on her lower lip and finally texted him back.

SENDING IT BACK, she punched in.

WRONG SIZE?

NO.

DON'T LIKE IT?

NO, NOT RIGHT.

Her phone signaled again with an incoming text message, but this time she turned the phone off. No doubt he would be knocking on her door next, wondering why she'd refused his thoughtful gesture. He'd be looking to make things right, for the pack and for them, which might not be for a while with the rafting trips scheduled for today. By the time Dan got off work at 6:00 p.m., she would be long gone to Arches National Park for an evening hike with God.

Jo packed up her day pack for the journey. In it went snacks, a water bottle, a hat, and sunglasses as the sun would still be quite bright in the height of summer. On a whim, she turned her phone back on to check the messages. Two more text messages came up, both from Dan, along with a voice mail from Todd. The text messages were:

WHAT'S NOT RIGHT?

WHAT'S WRONG?

And from Todd. "Hey, can you call me when you get this? I need to ask you a question." Good, as she also needed to ask him if she could borrow his car for the trip to Arches.

Todd was manning the desk when she called, wanting to check her numbers on an order sheet for the store. "So, how's your day off been?" he asked.

"Okay." She nearly spilled the beans about the backpack but decided to make it a nonissue. She planned to stop off at the post office anyway to mail it back. "I haven't been to Delicate Arch in a while, so I thought I'd take a hike there tonight. Can I borrow your car?"

"Sure. Man, I wish I could go with you, but there's too much to do here. I should lead a group into the Fiery Furnace again. You can make some good money with a hiking group."

Jo recalled how he liked to conduct hikes within Arches, and one being the famous but tricky labyrinth of trails within sandstone formations called the Fiery Furnace. "Don't you remember that one kid who got lost, and you had to call the rangers in to help find him?"

"You would remind me of that. Guess I'd better stick to rafting then. Anyway, have fun, don't get lost, and don't wreck my car."

"I don't plan to do either of the latter two. But I hope your insurance is good." She flipped closed the phone before he could issue a retort. Like she planned to smash his car into an arch or something. Wouldn't that make an interesting stunt—sending a car careening right through the South Window Arch. Jo sighed, put on her day pack, then lugged the large box toward the front door. This box was going to be a hassle, she had to admit. She'd have to come back home to pick up the box and fight traffic to take it to the post office before it closed. She decided to leave it for now. Maybe Dan would stop by and return it for her if she asked. Anything could happen.

When she stepped outside, heat like a blast furnace,

typical of a summer day in Utah, greeted her. It amazed her how wonderful air-conditioning felt when encountering these weather extremes. As usual, the town teemed with tourists. She waved to a few of the permanent residents who seemed like victims lost in this onslaught of tourism. But the residents also knew that tourism was their livelihood and never complained. Neither did she. Visitors brought in money, and money paid the bills.

Jo arrived at the shop to pick up Todd's car and saw Todd and Dan at the desk talking. Both of them looked up, but it was Dan's grin and large hazel eyes that she tried to ignore.

"Here you go," Todd said, surrendering his spare set of keys. "I filled up the tank today, too."

"Nice. Thanks so much."

"So where are you off to?" Dan asked.

"She's going to hike Delicate Arch," Todd said.

Jo tried to give Todd the evil eye, but he was looking in the opposite direction. *Great. Now Dan knows my plans.*

"Delicate Arch, huh?"

Todd continued. "It's fantastic at sunset. You should go see it, Dan. Why don't you take him along, Jolene? I'd feel better, anyway, if you didn't hike alone."

"I can take care of myself. I don't need an escort. I've done the trail plenty of times."

Todd gave her a strange look, accompanied by the look of expectation on Dan's face. She hesitated. "All right, c'mon," she said to Dan. "Better take water with you. Even though we're walking in the evening, it can still be in the nineties."

Dan obliged, grabbing some water and giving Todd a thumbs-up signal as if he'd just scored major points. Jo wasn't impressed by any of it. Nor did she want Dan tagging along. This was to be her hike, after all. Her and God. Once again,

Dan had wheedled his way into her life.

"I'd be glad to drive," he now said.

"That's okay. I know where to go. Easier than trying to navigate you through it all."

They said nothing until they entered the car. "Did you get my text messages? I left like a dozen," Dan said as she started the car.

"Look, if you're going to get into that, then please stay here. As it is, I wanted to do this hike alone."

Dan looked as if he'd been slapped. "Sorry I'm bothering you." He fumbled for the door handle.

"Wait. Don't worry about it, okay? I know we did talk about seeing Delicate Arch when you first got here. And it is nice at sunset. I just don't want to go into the text messaging thing. Or anything else, if that's okay. Can we call a truce?"

"Sure." Dan instantly relaxed, and the confident smile returned to his tanned face. His skin had begun to accept the extremes of Utah sun. At least he didn't look like the lobster of days past. He even looked like he'd lost a little weight. His upper arms were showing muscle. Jo wondered why she was examining him up close and personal like that. He then cast a small smile as if glad for her observing eye.

"So, what's wrong with the backpack?"

"I thought we weren't going to get into that." She blew out a sigh. "Okay, look. There's nothing wrong with it. I just don't think you should be buying me expensive presents."

"It's no big deal. It's just a way to say thank you for getting me the job with your cousin's company. For helping me learn all the ropes about cooking so I didn't look like a fool. For being there during our miracle day at the RV park. That kind of thing."

"It's still an expensive gift to be giving someone just for

doing the right thing."

Dan sat back, his fingers tapping on the door. "Jo, I had nowhere to go when I got here. You were the first friend I ran into. It's fine to give a friend a gift. At least, I thought it was. Maybe in Moab it's not."

Jo bit her lip, wondering if she had read too much into this whole deal. Dan obviously had money to burn and had tried to bless her. All she wanted to do was ship the gift back the moment she saw who it was from. Now she was glad that she hadn't dragged the box to the post office but had left it in the living room. Still, she had to wonder if something else lay hidden behind the high price tag and tough Cordura fabric. "Okay. I just think you spent too much."

"I have the money. In fact, I'm thinking of taking a new leap and buying a house." He withdrew a crumpled real estate brochure from his pocket. "The price has gone down, and it looks good. Has everything I want. And I've got enough money to put a decent down payment on it."

Jo glanced out the corner of her eye to see a picture of a humble, one-level ranch home. She recognized the area. "You have that kind of money on you?"

"Yeah. I left Virginia with my inheritance, so to speak. I mean, if you're going to start over somewhere else, might as well have enough money to do it with."

Jo turned onto the road leading into Arches National Park. "Do you want to stop at the visitor center?"

"Naw. You've seen one, you've seen them all."

Jo drove on, up the steep park road and into the bowels of red sandstone and tall rock formations. They bypassed Courthouse Rocks, boasting huge, house-sized boulders; passed Balanced Rock; and approached the turnoff for the Windows section, a series of arch formations. On a whim, Jo drove around the loop to observe Dan's reaction.

"Wow, this is amazing. I've never seen anything like it. I mean, to think that it took a million years of wind and water to carve these out." He began taking pictures on his cell phone. "Have to text these babies to Rob. Boy, will he be jealous!"

"It only takes God's finger to form an arch, you know. He doesn't need a million years to accomplish it."

He glanced over at her. "So you're one of those who doesn't believe the earth is a million years old?"

"I learned back in school how land can be altered in a moment's time. Like Mount St. Helens back in 1980, where two new lakes and a river valley were formed. It doesn't take God a zillion years to create something fantastic. It's just man's idea of what happened, to lessen the idea that there is a God."

"I don't know," Dan began dubiously as Jo drove back to the main park road. "Well, however the arches were made, they're still awesome."

Jo continued the drive as Dan stared out the window at the scenery until they arrived at the trailhead for Delicate Arch. She had to admit, she was enjoying his enthusiasm, as if everything was new and interesting to him. Maybe it was the Lord's doing that she'd changed her mind and allowed him to tag along. It made the time fun.

Once on the trail, Dan immediately began comparing the hikes he'd done in Virginia to the slippery sandstone beneath their feet and the red rocks and soil all around. It was like being on another planet, as he said. Jo listened to his chatter, thinking how nice it was to have a friend who enjoyed hiking as much as she. But could she count on Dan to keep this friendship status? Or was he looking to take advantage of the moment? If only she could be certain.

After negotiating the rock face, they found that the trail leveled off for a time before following a narrow ledge. In the distance, Jo could see the visitors gathered to take in the evening sunset. The thrill of expectation rose up within her.

"So how long does it take. . ." He never finished his statement. Instead his mouth dropped open. "Wow. Would you look at that? It's fantastic!"

Jo found a place on a nearby rock to watch the sun's fading rays make its final impression on the natural wonder of Delicate Arch. "It's best to come here this time of evening. You can see the arch so much clearer and even watch it change colors with the setting sun. See it turning from gold to orange and pretty soon, red."

Dan sat beside her on the rock, taking it all in. "I wish I had a better camera," he confessed. "Not sure how it's gonna come out on my cell phone. But better this than nothing, I suppose."

Jo sat quietly as the colors muted with the setting sun. What a wondrous spectacle made by God for His people to enjoy. It amazed her still every time she came here. And satisfied her with the knowledge that He was still at work in her life, creating something beautiful, even if it took time. The One who began the work in her life would complete it in the day of Christ Jesus.

All at once, Jo felt unexpected warmth settle around her. She tugged her gaze away from the beauty of Delicate Arch to find that Dan had slowly curled his arm around her. He tipped his head to one side as he looked at her. His eyes reflected the reddening skies above and the rocks below. He searched her face. He was going to kiss her, and to Jo's dismay, she was going to let him. At the last moment she turned away and stood to her feet, angry that she'd nearly slipped. "I need to head back before it gets too dark to see the trail." She grabbed her day pack, her feet moving swiftly as Dan hurried to keep up.

"Jo, I didn't mean anything. Sorry."

"You meant every bit of it, Dan. Life is like some game to you. I'm just one of your many playing pieces."

"No, you're not. Believe me, you're not. I wouldn't do anything to hurt you."

Jo stopped and whirled. "Well, you have hurt me. You said you wanted a friendship, but now I see what you're really after."

He paused also. "I do want a friendship. But, c'mon. We were enjoying a super sunset and a great view of the arch. It felt like the beach. What's a guy and a girl supposed to do on the beach at sunset?"

"Enjoy God's scenery without being taken advantage of," she retorted. "That's all I wanted to do, and you ruined it. Now I'm sorry I asked you along." She hurried on, knowing she could hardly outwalk him with his long legs and healthy male stamina. But she could definitely outwit him in other areas. Especially this game of the heart where he thought he was the master.

"Look, I'm sorry for what I did," he said again when they arrived back at the car. "You aren't going to drive off and leave me in the parking lot now, are you? It's a long hitch back to Moab."

"No, of course not. But you'd better take back that backpack of yours. It's not right."

He heaved a sigh. "Jo. . . ," he began.

"You can't just buy a relationship, Dan. And you aren't going to buy me. Or do anything else your devious mind is trying to think of right now. I like my life the way it is. I'm not looking for a relationship. So please, leave me alone."

They said nothing more the rest of the trip back to Moab. When Jo dropped the car off at the rafting center, they still had not spoken. Jo didn't care. It was better this way. She hurried to her place, nearly tripping over the box still sitting in the middle of the living room. Her phone signaled. It was a text message from Dan.

I'M SORRY.

I am, too, she thought. *Sometimes I just wish we'd never met. But sometimes I'm glad we did. . . .*

eight

Okay, so things were not as cool as Dan once thought. Not that anything was cool in this place. He asked Todd when the weather began to change, and he said not until late fall. Dan liked the fall season with the rich autumn colors and plenty of apples to pick at the nearby orchard. Then he reminded himself he wasn't in a color-changing, apple-picking place. Far from it. He was in Moab, Utah, the land of red rocks, canyons, and arches. The land where a feisty woman lived and now would have nothing to do with him.

Since the episode at Delicate Arch, he and Jo only spoke when necessary and mostly about business. A few days ago, he noticed on his credit card statement that the backpack had been returned. She said little to him about it or anything else. Yet Dan often thought about that evening jaunt they had taken to watch the sunset over Delicate Arch. He couldn't help himself, watching Jo perched on the rock, gazing at the spectacle before her with strands of her hair dancing around her shoulders. It was a ripe moment that had unfortunately turned a bit rotten. Maybe if he'd concentrated more on the friendship angle and not rushed things. Now she thought of herself as only a playing piece in his game of life, which she wasn't. She was so much more.

His thoughts turned to the rafting business. Things had changed drastically in the last few weeks, and it wasn't only in his relationship with Jo. Everything had changed since Todd decided to let Travis go after the life jacket incident.

Now that they were short one man, Dan found himself up to his neck in work. He had long since passed the river guide test and now was a fully licensed guide, among his other titles. He often arrived early in the morning to do the count that Travis once did. He did the river trips with gusto. Then he went home late at night after performing the same equipment check. He wondered why Todd didn't ask others on the workforce to do it, until it dawned on him that Todd trusted him. He'd developed a good enough reputation that Todd was giving him more and more responsibility. But with it, Dan felt himself beginning to drag under the weight of it. He yearned for free time to explore more of Moab and the surrounding area. Not that he wasn't outside enough. He'd done the river so many times, he knew it like the back of his hand. He'd even gone on a multiday excursion to Cataract Canyon, led by Todd. What a wild time that was, with Class IV and V rapids that dashed the rafts about like toy boats, to the delight of the college-aged gang that bought the trip. But Dan decided he preferred camping with families after witnessing the guy and girl entanglements on the college trip, complete with couples walking along the river and kissing behind the sagebrush. Without Jo, there was no sense thinking about kissing or anything else long term. He wouldn't put her in that kind of position even if he wanted. But why worry about it? She wouldn't have anything to do with him, period.

"Hey Dan, can I see you for a moment?" Todd called into the shop. Since it was now the middle of August, the number of trips was already beginning to wane as families returned home to get their kiddos into school. The river was running low, too, which affected the trips they conducted. Dan wondered how he would spend the winter without the usual work to keep him occupied. Maybe he would need to pick up a part-time job. Especially since he was seriously planning to buy that ranch home and had already begun the paperwork for the loan.

"Hey, Todd," Dan said, occupying a chair inside Todd's office. The place was typical of a single working guy, complete with awards for sporting competitions on the walls, a desk lined with empty sports drink bottles and crumpled potato chip bags, and samples of gear, such as sandals, water shorts, sunscreen, and even paddles propped up against the wall.

"The reason I asked you in here is to talk about your employment with Red Canyon Adventures."

Dan straightened. *Uh-oh.* Could Todd be giving him his pink slip? But why? He hadn't done anything wrong that he knew of. . .unless Jo spilled the beans about the Arches trip. Maybe Todd was angry he'd taken advantage of his innocent cousin—wooing her with a backpack and then trying to kiss her while watching the colors of Delicate Arch change in the setting sun.

"You know I had to fire Travis. So I was wondering if you might consider taking his place in the company. He was like my VP, if you think of it that way."

"I thought Jo was."

"Jo? You mean Jolene? Family name thing, I guess. She just joined the company to help me out. She's not looking for a managerial position. Travis had been here from the get-go and helped with arranging the trips and everything. Now that he's gone, I could use another guy for feedback on those kinds of things. Of course, I know you're still getting used to how the business is run, but I can tell you're a quick learner and you like what you do."

"Thanks." Dan had to wonder why Todd didn't ask any of

the other employees who had been here far longer than he. There must be something about him Todd liked, and that made him feel confident. "So what do I need to do?"

"I'll give you the details. Clue you in on the business part of the company. Let you in on decision making. But you're also still in learning mode, so this doesn't mean you get to run things. At least not yet." He added a grin.

"I wouldn't want to." But he did like the idea that someone thought him capable and trustworthy. Back home on Pop's peanut farm, Rob ran everything. Including Dan's life, it seemed. But Dan didn't feel the least bit intimidated by Todd. He found in him a certain camaraderie and a willingness to work together to make things happen. Not so back on the peanut farm. There it was a competition for his father's affection. Or maybe that was Dan's perception. Rob always seemed to win out in those instances. At dinner time, Pop praised Rob for one thing or another. Now at last Dan was making a name for himself. He was being promoted, even over others who had been there a lot longer. He planned to pin his new title on his chest for everyone to see.

"Don't tell me you're already nodding off on me, Dan," Todd said, staring at him. "It's not even 3:00 p.m."

"No, no, just thinking of home. How I never got a fair shake there, but here you trust me. Wish everyone thought as you do."

"I wish we could trust others. I mean, I trusted Travis, and he flat-out lied to my face. But I don't think you'd do that, Dan. You care about this business. I know you love the river, and the kids call you Raft Man. And that day with the missing PFDs, just to see your determination to make sure you came clean, well, that spoke volumes right there."

Dan must file that episode away for future reference. But

honestly, he did want to clear his name and make himself look good. What did he have if he didn't? A bad name is not what he came here for. But was trying to secure a good reputation good enough reason to abandon home and head for the red rocks? He grimaced at the thought.

Todd began going over some of the company records. Dan didn't know a whole lot about the business side of things, as Pop always took care of the paperwork. He did do some computer work for Pop, like the billing. Todd showed him the database of customers. He asked if he and Jo could do a mailing soon to prepare for next year. "We have to make sure we're up and running for the next season, even as this year is winding down."

"Yeah, it's hard to believe I've been here nearly three months. I guess that means this place is gonna change."

"Like how?"

"Well, for one, it won't feel like I'm stepping into the neighborhood pizza oven every time I leave my apartment."

"Moab does cool down," Todd said with a laugh. "We can get some snow, too. Of course, if you head four hours northwest of here, there's plenty of snow starting in a month or so near Salt Lake. The best skiing, too, at Park City. The Olympics were held there, you know."

Dan had done no skiing in his life and wasn't sure he wanted to learn.

"Jo loves to ski. She's first-rate."

Booyah. That sealed it. He'd learn to ski no matter what it took. And whatever else Jo liked to do. Though right now, he wasn't even sure they could get through the company mailer together without a major blowup. She was still angry over the Delicate Arch episode. Or he assumed she was angry as he hadn't heard much of anything from her except company business. There were no more tacos or nice drives or even runs to the store for food, which she did herself for the campouts. She was putting him on her ignore list. And the final slap was when she removed him from her friends list on Facebook.

Suddenly she appeared in the office doorway. "Hey Todd, I wanted to know. . ." She paused when her gaze leveled on Dan. Or rather she leveled two sets of blue daggers in the shape of crescents. Yep, she was still mad.

"C'mon in, Jolene. I was just telling Dan here about his new job. Since Travis is no longer with us, I have him taking up some of the company responsibility. And I need you two to work on the mailer soon.

One cheek muscle twitched in her otherwise smooth face. "Okay, fine. But I need to know if you plan to go out this afternoon as there's a family here who wants a rafting trip."

"I'll take them," Dan said happily.

"Can you go with him, Jolene? I still need to figure out some things here with the files."

"Yeah, sure." Jo marched out.

Dan followed, peeking into the store to see Mom, Dad, and several young boys pleading with the parents to buy them each new kids' sunglasses. "Looks like fun," he commented.

"Just remember, we're here to do a job," she told him. "We're taking the family rafting, and that's it. You take advantage of this situation, and I'll make sure Todd knows all about it."

"Understood, ma'am." He even saluted for effect.

Jo rolled her eyes and strode off to gather the PFDs and other equipment. Dan met the family in the rear of the store and told them briefly where they would be going and some safety pointers.

"Are we going out in the boat soon?" asked one of the boys.

"Real soon. And here's my assistant." He acknowledged Jo. "We're going to take you over in the van to the drop-off point to begin the trip. And you're in luck. You'll have your own private guides, the two of us."

"So you and your wife are taking us?" asked the mother.

Dan looked out the corner of his eye to see Jo's face blanch. "We're just co-workers, ma'am," Dan said swiftly

"Oh, I'm sorry. I thought maybe you were a husband and wife team. You seem to work well together."

Thank you, God! You're making my day big-time. This couldn't have begun any better, even if the look on Jo's face told him otherwise. It wasn't as if he'd paid the mom money to say that. He shrugged in Jo's direction as if to communicate, Hey, don't blame me; I didn't set them up.

She turned away.

❧

The rafting venture went smoothly. Dan liked seeing the way Jo tackled the trip. She had good strength and know-how of the river. When they arrived back at the shop, he decided one compliment shouldn't throw her off too badly. "You were good out there today. Did you see the nice tip the family gave us?"

She pushed back strands of hair from her face. "Yeah. Thanks."

"Maybe we should spend it on a nice, thick steak. And onion rings. What do you say?"

She shook her head. "No thanks."

Dan hesitated. Suddenly he felt the urge to say something, anything to calm the tension between them. "Look, I'm really sorry about what happened on the hike the other night. I should've never done what I did. I mean, I broke your trust.

It wasn't what you bargained for."

"No, it wasn't. I just wanted to have a good time with God, and you had to move on in. And the problem is, I nearly gave in. I don't like that."

Dan tried to hide his utter delight at this revelation. *She almost gave in? She wanted to kiss me, too? She has feelings for me? Yeah!*

"Dan, you need to know there's more to life than you. There's a much bigger picture here. Other people have feelings, and they're trying to do what's right in life."

"I know that."

"Do you? I know you say we're friends, and you're just helping. But then you move in like the doors are wide open. Even if I was tempted to give in, I won't do it. I'm not that kind of person. You may have come from the open arena of dating with any girl that pops along. But I would rather wait on God to bring the right man into my life."

God does that kind of thing? Since when? Dan never equated the God of the stained-glass window to a God who cared about a person's relationship status. Jo made God sound so. . . personal. "Don't tell me you've never been in a relationship."

Jo hesitated. "Yes, I have. And maybe that's why I've decided not to go shopping around the neighborhood. It hurts too much. I'd rather wait on God and see where He leads me. He's never let me down. He knows what's best for me."

Dan thought about it. How often did he think that God had let him down? Except now when God seemed to be smiling everywhere Dan turned. All but this one small problem standing before him. "I still don't see the problem in spending our nice tip on a steak or taking a walk or watching a sunset on a trail."

"But you saw firsthand what happens when you even try to do the most innocent of things. Like taking a hike to see Delicate Arch, and you take the opportunity to make your move."

"Look, it's a guy thing. I didn't mean anything by it, and I sure didn't mean for it to upset you. If it makes you feel any better, I promise it won't happen again." He watched Jo remove her hair band and allow her hair to flow free. He sighed. Maybe he wasn't being totally honest. If he saw Jo by another sunset and with her hair blowing in the breeze like that, he probably would try to kiss her again. But right now he was willing to say anything to stem the flow of anger until things changed. And he believed they would in time. Todd was making him one of the head honchos. He and Jo would be working more and more together. It would naturally flow that they would get to know each other, and with that would follow a closer relationship. He just had to learn to put the brake on and not do a free fall that would scare her away. "If I promise to be on good behavior and be a friend, can you accept a friendship?"

Jo hesitated. "Look, I don't want to seem tyrannical or something. I just want to guard my heart. And you should guard yours, too, Dan. Unless you don't care about it. Obviously you aren't a one-woman kind of guy."

That comment stung. No, he couldn't say that Jo was his first interest. She was about the sixth, maybe, counting the girls he knew back in high school. And then his two-year stint on the community college scene with Lenora before financial necessity brought him back to the peanut field. But none of those girls had the kind of principles Jo did. Or her stubbornness when it came to her religion. Like thinking God was a matchmaker, of all things! That really threw him for a loop.

"But I will spend a little of the tip on ice cream," she suddenly announced.

Dan spun about and stared. "You will? Great! I mean, okay."

She laughed. "Besides, we have business to discuss. With Travis gone, there are some things I probably should go over with you since you're basically taking his place."

"Todd has been doing that."

"Well, other things. What to expect in your new role, working with Todd. It takes a lot to keep things going, Dan. And it has to be taken seriously."

He nodded. *Get serious, Dan.* He needed to do it on the job front as well as in this relationship. No more games. No more kid stuff. Time to act like a man. Whatever that meant.

❧

"Well, we made it through," Dan said with a smile, sitting back to allow the banana split to slowly digest.

"Made it through what?"

"A nice dessert without blowups, confusion, or misinterpretations. Just straight talking." He watched her scrape the last bit of chocolate syrup from the sundae cup. He averted his gaze while she licked the spoon to watch other customers coming in and out. Suddenly he straightened in his chair and stared. His ice cream turned to a cold rock in his stomach.

"What's the matter?"

"Travis and Chris just walked in the door. Wouldn't you know it? I swear they must have homing beacons attached to their baseball caps. Like those little lights I've seen." He looked around to see if the store had a rear exit. No such luck. And no luck either in the nonrecognition department as Chris strode over, hands in his pockets, a grin parked on his face.

"Hey, I just wanted to thank you two."

"For what?" Dan said before feeling Jo's foot nudge his shinbone.

"For giving me Travis. He's excellent."

"Well, you'd better watch it. He also takes shortcuts and tells tall tales." Again he felt Jo poke him and shake her head.

"Oh yeah, and let's get on the topic of telling outright tales, shall we? Like the salmonella lie? I'm sure you don't want me to go there, Jolene, do you?"

"Look, we were just leaving, Chris. Glad Travis is working out in your company. He didn't with us, and that's fine." She took up her backpack purse and stood to her feet.

Dan had no intention of leaving, not when he saw Travis already beginning his manipulation tactics on Chris through fancy storytelling. Until he felt the pressure of Jo's hand on his arm, urging him to leave. He looked over at Travis to see a smile on his face that grated his nerves.

Outside the shop, he whirled to face her. "Why did you drag me out of there like I'm some kid?"

"Because if we didn't leave, you were looking to start a brawl. All that's needed is a few accusations to fly, and then it begins. Chris was baiting us both. You just have to stop taking the bait."

"I don't care. You can see Travis has been filling Chris's head with lies about the company. Doesn't that bother you?"

"So what if he has? It won't go anywhere."

Dan couldn't believe her calmness in the midst of this battle. He wanted to fight. His manly muscles were crying out for it. But somehow he allowed the soothing balm of Jo to calm the tide. With reluctance, he walked away.

"Now do you feel better?"

"No, because that guy is still sitting there, lying through his teeth."

"Dan, the only person he's hurting is himself."

"How did this whole salmonella thing with Chris come about anyway? He mentioned it again. I remember you telling me about it when I first got here."

She let out a sigh. "We heard complaints from several people that they had become sick soon after a rafting trip using Chris's company. Of course, whenever you hear of a stomach bug mixed with food, you think salmonella. Well, Todd questioned the possibility. The rumor leaked out. Chris lost business, and state health inspectors even showed up. He was cleared of the allegation, but the damage had been done."

Dan sighed. "I don't know, but I'm worried. Chris isn't going to forget what happened. And with Travis there, adding in his bad feelings about Todd, I smell trouble."

"Then you need to pray about it, Dan. It's all you can do."

Pray about it. What a strange concept. Maybe he should. But he really didn't know the One he would be praying to. Not like Mom and Pop did. Or Jo even. Just the mere thought made him feel uncomfortable. No, he'd put the praying aside and let Jo take over that part. Instead, he'd spend the rest of the evening thinking about the company and how to keep Chris and Travis from showing up on the company's front doorstep when they least expected it.

nine

The activity at the rafting center slowly began to die down after Labor Day. As vacationers went back to work and students to school, there was less and less demand for trips during the week. Weekends still proved busy, but Jo could take a day or two off midweek to do the things she wanted. And those days didn't amount to much. The laptop became her friend. She sometimes gathered with friends she knew from church. She thought about taking up some kind of craft and even bought a card-making kit, thinking it might be nice this year to give out handmade cards for Christmas.

Jo turned on the laptop to see what was happening. Once again, Dan asked for a friend request on the social network. Ever since she'd taken him off her friends list after the escapade at Arches, he inquired if he could come back. And each time she hit the Ignore feature. Until today, when she felt in a more jovial mood and accepted. After she hit the button to access his profile page, she noticed the new picture of him making some strange face while sitting in the raft. She wondered then about his background. She still knew so little about him. Why he really left Virginia to come here. What his plans were in life. If he would ever consider putting God in the equation.

The chat box popped up. I STRUCK OIL, Dan wrote.

WHAT DO YOU MEAN YOU STRUCK OIL?

I MEAN I'VE BEEN TRYING TO GET YOUR ATTENTION NOW FOR WEEKS. DID YOU KNOW I'VE CLOSED ON MY HOUSE? AND

I'M HAVING AN OPEN HOUSE THIS FRIDAY NIGHT. LIKE TO HAVE YOU COME IF YOU CAN.

Jo thought about it. Like her social calendar was booked these days. I'LL HAVE TO SEE. YOU CAN'T HAVE TOO MANY PEOPLE COMING TO IT. YOU DON'T KNOW THAT MANY IN MOAB.

TRUE. JUST EMPLOYEES FROM THE COMPANY. MAYBE I SHOULD INVITE OUR ARCHENEMIES.

Jo could imagine the confrontation if Chris and Travis showed up. Thankfully, after the ice-cream encounter several weeks ago, things had been quiet. No more chain rattling.

YOU KNOW BETTER THAN THAT, she typed.

I KNOW. I HAVE YOU TO STRAIGHTEN ME OUT.

Jo thought on that one. She remembered that tonight was their young adult fellowship at the church. Well, why not? HEY, SINCE YOU LIKE PARTIES SO MUCH, COME ON OVER TO THE GATHERING AT MY CHURCH TONIGHT. WE'RE GOING TO PLAY BOARD GAMES.

WHAT TIME?

8:00.

I'M THERE.

That was easy, Jo thought, reminding her of the commercial with the same slogan. She grimaced and closed the laptop, wondering what she had just gotten herself into. Had she opened herself up to more trouble? She thought not. This was a good group to join. Dan needed to see how Christian guys and girls interacted with each other. He could use basic lessons on what it means to have a real relationship with the Lord. Not engaging in romantic encounters at every bend in the road, but serving each other and waiting on God for Him to open the doors. She smiled, thinking of it more like a trap to capture Dan's soul than anything. *Hope you're ready, dear ol'*

Dan, she thought smugly.

Jo arrived early that evening to clue the group leaders in on the coming intrusion by Dan Mallory. They were a married couple named Brian and Trish. "He's a transplanted Virginian who isn't sure what he supposed to do in life," she told them. "And he's Todd's assistant in the company."

"We look forward to meeting him," Brian said with a smile.

The meeting soon came to order. Brian led the group in prayer and asked for testimonies and prayer requests. Jo glanced at her watch. No sign of Dan. Jo tapped her foot, feeling her agitation rising. How she wanted him here to listen to the testimonies and find out what was happening in other people's lives.

A half hour later, just as Brian was bringing out the games, Dan showed up. Jo tried not to let her irritation get the better of her, but she did wonder if he'd planned all along to avoid the first part of the meeting. She went ahead and introduced Dan to Brian.

"So are you settled here in Moab?" Brian asked.

"Sure am. Just got myself a nice place, too. Wheels. A job. Life's been real good. It's been a blessing for sure."

Jo tried not to bristle as Dan smoothly threw out a few colloquial Christian expressions. He went on to tell Brian about God's blessing over his life ever since he arrived here and how he'd wanted to meet other people. "So this is a real answer to prayer."

I wonder when's the last time you really prayed, Dan? She looked to Brian to see if he could read through it all. Brian only smiled and invited him to play a game. Dan looked to Jo and asked what she would be doing. When she mentioned entering the Monopoly challenge, Dan agreed to play also. But now she wasn't in the mood to do anything. Especially having Dan sitting right next to her at the table, flashing a smile now and then, and using Christian lingo with everyone around him.

God, can't people see who he is?

And then a still, small voice responded. *"Who is he?"*

The question startled her. *He's just pretending, to get what he wants.*

"Like someone else I know."

Jo sat stunned, even as Dan gave her the dice and told her it was her turn. She looked at the board game and rolled the dice, all the while wondering if she, too, had been playing the game of Christianity. Throwing dice and moving her piece to get ahead. As it was, she didn't leave Virginia on the right foot. She left because of personal things she'd never revealed to anyone but Brian and Trish, and of course, Todd. She thought she'd made the right decision when she did it, but was she running instead of confronting the past? Pretending to play the game without reconciliation?

"You aren't into this anymore, are you?" Dan asked.

"No, not really." She looked around and found another woman, Meg, to take her place at the table. She walked off, catching Dan's thoughtful gaze as he continued to play the game. Life was too confusing. She'd been rebuked at her own game of life, it seemed.

"What's up, Jo?" Trish asked, coming up to her. "Is it Dan?"

"Dan isn't a Christian, Trish, but he's pretending like he is."

"The only one who really knows his heart is God, right?"

"Yes, but. . .I don't know. He's looking to be more than just friends with me. I've tried to hold him off, but there are nice things about him."

"You did the right thing by bringing him here. Sometimes when we get away from a church family and strike out on our own, temptations happen we don't expect. Getting him involved with other Christian guys is a good way to go. Hopefully he can come to church on Sunday."

"That may be difficult right now as many of the rafting trips are still going strong on weekends. But when the fall season ends, he should be able to come."

"That would be even better. But you do what you need to guard your heart, Jo. Give it over to God. Let Him continue to work through you. And feel free to have Brian intervene with Dan whenever you need him to. He's glad to help."

"Thanks." With Dan still immersed in the game, Jo decided this was a good time to disappear. Hopefully Dan would make new friends and set his sights on other things rather than her. And she could finish her own soul-searching and seek to discover what she needed to resolve in her life.

❧

Jo was happy with the way things were going. There had been a distinct change in Dan ever since she introduced him to her young adult group. To her surprise, he was faithful to come every Wednesday night, even though he often ran late, avoiding much of the prayer and testimony time. Yet she was encouraged to find him interacting with other brothers in the Lord and making friends.

The rafting season had ended and life turned quiet. She and Dan spent workdays doing inventory, mailing out brochures for upcoming business, and checking out new stock for the store. The cooler temperatures brought out long-sleeved shirts and jeans from the closet. When a faint dusting of snow painted the red rocks, Dan was out there with his cell phone camera, taking shots of it. He continued to remain courteous with her. Things were definitely looking better.

"So are you coming?" Todd asked her one day as she was counting out sunglasses on the counter.

"Of course. Why would I miss your New Year's Eve party?"

"Just wondering. You seem so quiet these past few months. Are you upset?"

"About what?"

"That I made Dan my assistant in the company instead of you. I know you've been here longer and all. In fact, you've essentially become part of the company in many ways."

"Believe me, I don't want the aggravation of being a VP."

Todd whistled a sigh. "Okay, good. I just thought maybe you were mad at me or something." He paused. "By the way, do you ever hear from Ross?"

Jo froze when he mentioned her older brother. "No, actually I haven't. Why would you bring that up?"

He shrugged. "I don't know. With the holidays and all, you start thinking about family."

"I'm sorry your mom isn't here anymore." She saw a pall come over his face, as he recalled how his mother died in a car crash a few years back and how his dad had nothing to do with him. *Why were there all these family difficulties in life?* she wondered, thinking of her own falling out, not only with Ross but with her parents, too.

"I think about her around Christmas. But hey, we're family now. Cousins, anyway. I'll let you get back to your counting."

Jo watched him move off to the office. He was being melancholic again, like her, thinking of family and all that they had lost. If only they could gain something back. But she had no plans yet to get in touch with her brother Ross or her parents. Ross had made life a challenge in so many ways, being the proverbial older brother by telling her what to do and where to go. Saying it was his responsibility to take care of her, especially with their vast differences in ages. Fifteen years to be exact. She didn't want to let on to anyone, especially Dan, of her troubled years as a teen. Having to leave home and move in with Ross when her parents couldn't deal with her. Ross was the only one who opened his door to her. And what did she do? Left him, too. Dan didn't realize she wasn't a Goody Two-Shoes. She'd had tough breaks in life. But all that was better kept locked away for now.

Jo heaved a sigh and stared at the pile of sunglasses. Now she would have to recount them with all these distractions. Why did these things have to come to the surface now? She'd received acceptance and counseling when she first came here. She'd found forgiveness for what she had done in the past and moved on with life. But now the past was coming back to haunt her. Maybe because she was being nitpicky and judgmental of Dan.

"What's up?" She heard a cheery voice call out.

Dan arrived with a grin parked on his face, looking as if he'd conquered the world.

"Sunglasses." She modeled one for him. "Rather, counting them."

"Wow, that is too sweet. So, are you going to Todd's party?"

"Of course. I'm his cousin. I do the serving."

"You gonna wear a little waitress outfit?"

Jo's face heated, and she looked away.

"Sorry. That was a tactless comment." He stepped back, the cheerfulness evaporating from his face. "Moab looks like a great place to celebrate Christmas though."

Jo moved sunglasses from one pile to another. "Dan, do you ever think about your family?"

"My family? Of course. Why?"

"Just wondering, with it being Christmas and all."

"Actually, I've been trying to figure out what to give them this year. I thought about giving them free tickets to a rafting trip next year. Rob would love it. I mean, I've got the money to fly them out. I just don't see my mom heading down the Colorado in a raft." He leaned over with his elbows resting on the counter. "How about yours?"

"Well, Todd is having the party, so we exchange gifts then."

"No, I mean your family. Mom, Pop, brothers, sisters."

"They. . .they're in New York. Except for my oldest brother."

"I went to New York City once. Saw all the famous places. Went up the Empire State Building. Saw the Statue of Liberty. And of course, the footprints of the Twin Towers. That was a sobering moment."

"Uh. . .sorry, I really need to get back to counting these."

"Oh, sure." He looked at her thoughtfully before moving on toward Todd's office. Jo didn't want to relive the rest of the story, that she'd not seen her family since she was fifteen, that she'd been cared for by her brother for several rough years until fleeing to Moab. That she'd put her family through worse fiery furnaces than anything Arches National Park could dish out on their Fiery Furnace trail. That she likely still nursed some unresolved guilt for gumming up her life and theirs. For thinking they had raised a model daughter, only to find her caught up in drugs and a crude boyfriend. *God, why is all this coming out now? It's been safely buried away for so long. Are You trying to do something by resurrecting this? But why now, and why with Dan around?* Maybe because she wanted to appear the solid Christian to him. That he wouldn't know the down and dirty parts, that she wasn't all she was cracked up to be, at least before she came to know the Lord.

For now, Jo settled herself into the Christmas festivities. Todd closed down the shop for two weeks. Jo got out her ski equipment and took off for a day on the slopes near Salt Lake to be by herself and think. When she turned her cell phone on, there were at least a dozen messages from Dan asking where she went. She grimaced, feeling no inclination to give him daily updates on her life, especially when she was trying to sort things out.

Jo brushed out her hair and put on a shiny top and black jeans for the New Year's Eve party. Todd always threw a nice bash at his place, with great food and plenty of soda—though he did have beer for the drinking crowd. She planned to be in the kitchen helping wherever she could. And staying out of Dan's sight, even though he'd been on good behavior these many weeks.

Jo arrived at Todd's. The place twinkled with strings of multicolored lights lingering from the Christmas holiday. With the warm evening, many gathered out on the front porch, sipping whatever was in their glasses and talking. Jo slipped by, giving swift greetings, and entered the kitchen. Dan stood at the counter, making an hors d'oeuvre tray. "What are you doing in here?"

"Todd asked me to help out. He likes my flair for arranging food. What do you think?"

Jo liked the way he had arranged the crackers and cheese to spell out the New Year. "Very creative."

"Thanks." He stood there for a moment, gazing at her, looking as if he liked what he saw.

Jo felt her face grow warm. She hurried out to find Todd and see if anything else needed to be done.

"Don't worry about it," he told her. "Just have fun. Dan's my cook tonight."

Super. She tried not to read into it and grabbed a soda instead. There were several hours left to wade through before the stroke of midnight. She wondered how she would pass the time. She wandered outside to find the moon had risen, bathing the landscape in a drapery of white. It looked peaceful, as if God would bring His peace on the upcoming year. How she needed to embrace the way of peace, especially with what He'd been doing in her heart these past few weeks. She sipped her soda, thinking of the Christmas card she'd received from Ross. It was simple and friendly, asking how she was and telling her they were thinking of her. Even Dad and Mom had sent one, as well as a gift card to some store that she would have to drive to Salt Lake to shop in. At least they were thinking of her.

Just then she felt someone touch her arm. Dan came up, holding a small plate of food. "Got you some of these before everyone else dives in. Sausage balls, cheese, and crackers."

"Thanks, but I'm not hungry."

He put the plate down. "Jo, you've seemed lost now for a while. What's going on?"

"I don't know. Just thinking." Her gaze encompassed the velvety rocks once more. "I'm glad I'm here in Moab."

"Me, too. I mean, I think of Pop and Mom. You know, this is the first holiday I've spent away from them?"

"Was it hard?"

"Not as bad as I thought. I talked to them on Christmas Day. I think Mom was crying on the phone, but I couldn't tell. Rob said he liked the idea of going rafting sometime. Pop was pretty quiet, except to ask how I was getting along. Told me he was praying for me. That kind of thing."

"That's good. It's good that your family cares about you."

"Jo, I care about you, too." His fingers began to sweep her

forearm. "I think about you all the time."

"Dan. . ."

"It's almost the New Year. I would really like to make a resolution."

"So would I."

His hazel eyes reflected the moon. "You would?"

"Uh-huh. Never to be alone with you at sunset or in the moonlight. It's not a good idea."

"Jo, c'mon. Stop playing."

"Playing?"

"Look, I've played along now for a while. I went to your church group and all. But let's be honest. You know you've got feelings for me. You said so yourself not that long ago. It's getting kind of boring waiting for you to come around. Let's just make a resolution this year to spend more time together."

Jo felt the anger rising up within her. "Hey Dan, I've got an even better suggestion."

"Yeah?" He drew closer, the look on his face betraying his desire to kiss her. His arms began to curl around her.

"I'm into a totally new game for the New Year."

"Sounds good. Just let me know the rules." He began to nuzzle her neck.

"Okay. It's called Hands Off. I mean it." She pushed him away and hurried off. She walked fast, away from the merrymaking all around Moab, and headed straight for her apartment. *Oh God, how I hate the mess I'm in. With love. With life. I pray this will be a year of new beginnings. That somehow my life will count for something. Things can be made new again. But, please, leave Dan out of my life right now.*

ten

Love is supposed to be thicker than water. He'd heard it from an oldies song somewhere. He wanted it like the flour and water paste he used back in grade school to glue projects together. But nothing could paste this relationship back together, as much as he wanted. Love was too runny right now, running right out of his life. It did not bind them together. In fact, it was nonexistent, though Dan could say with his heart that he was falling head over heels in love with Jo. But since the last few episodes, she'd once more resorted to ignoring him. She'd hardly spoken to him except to pass on something from Todd. There were no more ice-cream socials or other gatherings. At least she did show up at the game night Wednesday nights at her church, but she made certain she didn't play the same game as he. For a time he stopped going to the event in a protest of sorts, but after a while, he missed the camaraderie. He liked hanging out with this bunch. They were interesting and godly. He hoped that if he continued to hang out with Jo and her friends, she would warm up to him.

But as usual, he let his feelings get in the way of his plans, and now he was back to square one. Or rather he seemed to be flirting with the negative region. At least he was secure in other areas of life. He enjoyed having his own house. Work was okay though quiet. He spent his free time exploring Moab to see all that there was to see. Like walking the river walk. Cruising the outdoor shops. And yes, enduring other run-ins with Travis and Chris when he inadvertently stumbled upon their rafting center. He should have remembered the name of the place when he entered it, but it had slipped his mind until he saw them.

"What are you doing here, Dan?" Travis immediately called out. "Scoping out our place for Todd?"

"It was purely accidental. I was just seeing what Moab had to offer. I didn't know this was Chris's place."

"Sure. Nice try."

Dan tried to exit, but it seemed Travis was more interested in conversation. He asked how the company was doing. If Todd had received any bad news lately—though Dan couldn't begin to figure out what *that* meant. So Dan decided to change the subject slightly and loosen up the talk. "The only grim news I've got to report is the girl angle. Jo doesn't seem interested in me no matter what I do. Guess I don't have it or something. Any thoughts on the subject, guys?"

His question brought the reaction he'd hoped. The talked turned from his place of employment to girls. Chris began to relate about his past and present girlfriends. Travis said Jo didn't look at anyone or anything. "But she's got quite a past, so what do you expect?"

This comment piqued Dan's interest. "What do you mean by that? I mean, we all have sordid pasts in one form or another."

"Oh, why she left New York and then Virginia and all. I mean, she originally left home when she was fifteen. Or rather her parents kicked her out from what I hear."

Dan tried not to look interested, but on the inside he was riveted. He pretended to study a rack of water shorts, hoping and praying that Travis would continue to run his mouth. And he did for a time, talking about how she moved in with her older brother in Virginia, but even he couldn't deal with her. "She's got an attitude, and now she walks around holier-than-thou when she's messed up. Can't figure out how getting religious all of a sudden makes you perfect."

Dan was intrigued. Why was Jo kicked out at age fifteen? It never dawned on him that she would have any troubles in life. She seemed so. . .well, perfect and pretty. And holy, as Travis said, like trying to stay holy in her relationships. The more he thought about it, the more curious he became.

Back home, Dan opened his laptop to check Facebook. Once again Jo had dumped him as a friend on the social network after the New Year's incident. Round Two. He wished there was some way to look into her heart and see what was happening. It would be nice to know she also struggled with things. They would be so good for each other, helping each other through the tough parts of life. Wasn't Pastor Brian just saying the other day that lessons learned from troubling times can help someone else?

He closed the laptop with a decisive click. Now he had an overwhelming desire to help Jo with her past. She'd helped him when he first got here, and now he wanted to do something in return. At least be there for her. Though he knew what would happen if he tried to intervene. She would push him away with the "Hands Off" game again. *Jo, I wish you could understand that I care about you. Okay, so I like you, too. I like being with you. I would very much like to kiss you, even though it's probably not a good thing right now. But I care. I'm not just out for your body or something, even if you are good-looking. I care about you personally. And if you're in trouble, I want to help.*

Wow, what a unique concept. He wasn't thinking about himself for a change. He was finally getting the eyes off Dan

Mallory and onto someone else. Considering someone else's feelings instead of harping on his own.

Dan checked his hair and appearance today. He wanted to look his best but not appear as if he were trying to play up the moment. He chose a long-sleeved polo shirt and cargo pants. And for kicks he added a Bible, one Mom gave him when he turned sixteen. How she dearly wanted him to read it. Dan never opened it. Now it would make a good prop for this meeting. Maybe he could go on the guise of needing some kind of biblical lesson. He tried to think of something Pastor Brian said that he could use to pose a question. That would appear innocent enough. And then he could find out more about her in the process and especially her past. Patience was the key to turning love into glue. And when they did come together, he would let nothing tear them apart.

He arrived at Jo's apartment to see a light shining in the window. *Good, she's home.* He came to the door and heard singing. He wasn't familiar with the tune, something about God and the need to go deeper or something. He paused for a few minutes to listen. She had a nice voice. He looked at the Bible he held, thinking he ought to do his own deep searching sometime.

He knocked. The singing continued. He knocked harder. It suddenly stopped and there came the patter of footsteps.

"No way, Dan." He heard the muffled response behind the door.

Great, she can see through the security hole. "Jo, this will only take a minute. I've got a question about what Pastor Brian said Wednesday night."

"Look, I know that game. Pretend to have a question when your real motive is to find a way inside. Forget it."

Man, she did know everything. She must have lived on the other side of the tracks. "Okay, look, I'm concerned about you."

She didn't respond.

"Travis said you'd been through things when you were younger, how your parents made you leave and all. I—I just wanted to let you know if you ever want to talk about it. . ."

The door suddenly burst open. He jumped back and nearly dropped the Bible.

"What in the world is Travis doing blabbing about my personal life to you?"

Dan sensed the water getting quite hot. "We were just talking about relationships and all. He said you'd been in some tough situations when you were a teen."

"Todd!" she shouted, stomping her foot. "He must have said something to Travis. For crying out loud, it's *my* personal life. So Todd told Travis, and Travis told you. What's next, the *National Enquirer*? And no, I'm not some Hollywood star's ex-lover or an alien from outer space. And yes, I did have a tough time as a teen. Who doesn't?"

"I know." He saw then she was staring at the Bible he carried. The next thing he knew, he was standing inside her apartment for the first time. It was a nice place, too. Lots of feminine touches. Magenta curtains. Framed prints of puppies. A clock hanging on the wall with numerals in the shape of rosebuds. Totally girlish but sweet. How could this woman have any problems? She was sweet, kind, tenderhearted, fabulous-looking. . .

Jo flopped down on the sofa. "I just don't understand why people have to go telling everyone their life's history. And of course, now you know mine."

"Well, not really. Only that you've had a tough time.

I mean, being a teen these days is not easy. Lots of peer pressure."

"Tell me about it. That's all I've had. Pressure coming from every direction. And James was a total idiot."

James? Dan tried not to look interested, but he was very interested, especially if there was another guy in the picture.

"I should've never gotten involved with that guy." She paused. "Maybe you need to understand why I don't care to date or hang out with guys. You see, a guy ruined my life. Or rather, I let him ruin my life. He got me involved with drugs. My family kicked me out. They said they couldn't deal with it, that I needed to go live with my brother Ross who had a better handle on things, being older. Then Ross kicked me out, too. Well, that's not true. I kicked myself out. I came here to find a new life. Then I got involved in the church here. Brian and some of the others helped me. I got saved. And now I have a new outlook on life."

Dan tried to absorb all this, but he must have had a stunned expression on his face, because Jo wriggled her nose.

"So I'm not the queen of the castle as you thought, huh? I've got faults."

"Well, who doesn't?"

"I don't know. You seem to think you have your act together."

"I do, don't I?" He laughed shortly. "No one's perfect. But sometimes it's good to start over again. I couldn't stand where I was either. Moab seems to be the place where people find help. I mean, you've helped me so much. And I'm sorry I keep trying to take advantage of it."

She sat massaging a sofa pillow with her fingertips, a move that distracted him. He inhaled a sharp breath and looked away, back to the rosebud clock. Boy, would Mom love a clock like that.

"Yeah, you sure have," she finally said. "And I'm still not convinced you aren't trying to do the same thing now. So with that. . ." She stood to her feet and went to the door. "I hope you don't mind me asking you to leave now."

"Okay, sure. I just wanted you to know that you can always talk to me."

She said nothing more. He left, wondering if anything had been accomplished this night. One thing was certain. He really didn't know the true Jolene at all.

❧

Dan felt better about the situation with Jo, but not about work. Something was definitely eating Todd. He'd not been right for several weeks now. He'd lost his friendliness, his zing for things, and the way he used to invite Dan into his office to talk about stuff. And then there was supposed to be all the planning for the upcoming season, which Todd had done little of since the winter mailer. All of this concerned Dan. Especially when he got a call from Todd that he didn't need to come to work for a few days. Sometimes things were slow, and he wasn't needed. But days off in the spring when stuff should be moving left him wondering what was afoot. He called Jo to ask what was happening, but she offered little in the way of information. He thought about the last few outings on the river but could think of nothing he'd done wrong. Maybe he was just being paranoid.

He decided to be of good cheer anyway, despite his reservations, and walked into the shop whistling. He didn't bother to notice the CLOSED sign on the front door. Jo should be at the cash register, ready for the day, but she was strangely absent. In fact, the place didn't feel or look right. He walked to the back of the shop and looked in Todd's office. He saw Evan, one of the other employees, walk past him with his head down.

"Hey Evan, what's up, man?"

Evan ignored him. A strange feeling came over Dan. He peeked into the office again to see Todd running his hand through his hair. Todd looked up and flinched when he saw Dan. "Well, you'd better get in here."

Dan looked at his watch as he slipped into a chair. "I know I'm a little late. Where's Jo?"

"Dan, we've got a major problem." He smacked some papers on his desk. "We've been served with a lawsuit."

"What?"

"Yeah, by one of the customers that went on a trip early last season. I don't know if you recall, but you were learning to help guide on that trip. It's from the girl who fell in the river."

"You mean earring girl?" Dan thought back to the conversation she had with her boyfriend on the bus. *And if I fall in, I'm suing*. She wasn't kidding.

"I have insurance, but as you know with the economy and everything, it's been getting tough. And this girl's got a top-notch lawyer who's trying his best to find loopholes in the agreements each of the customers sign. It seems she's a state representative's daughter."

This was going from bad to worse.

"You should have treated her with kid gloves," Todd added.

"How was I to know that? I mean, it was my first day on the job. Travis was in charge of the boat."

Todd again ran his fingers through his hair. "Well, whatever. But this is going to kill me once word gets out. And it already has."

"Just fight it."

"Easier said than done. You know how much this will cost me in business and money? Especially with her kind of lawyer. She's claiming she got some kind of neck injury from the fall. Had to wear a neck brace. Even though customers are supposed to take responsibility for what happens according to the disclaimer they sign, they're claiming that because an unlicensed guide was at the helm, the paper she signed is null and void."

Dan flew to his feet and began to pace. *I don't believe this!* "She's making all this up. She wasn't hurt."

"Even if she is, I don't see how we can win in the long run. She'll play the innocent girl, and she'll get sympathy. And then witnesses saw you at the helm when the boat hit a rock and she fell out."

Dan whirled. "Todd. . .I. . ."

"Look, Dan, there isn't anything else to say. But this is your notice. I'm going to have to let you go. I can't have you here with this going on. Even if Travis was there with you, he's already gone."

Dan attempted a sick chuckle of disbelief, but inside he felt like he was dying. "You've got to be kidding."

"No, I'm deadly serious. I don't know how I'm gonna keep going as it is. Especially when word of this gets out."

This was a nightmare come true. "Todd, I don't know what to say."

"There's nothing you can say. It was my fault for putting you out there on your first day. It was a dumb thing to do. Even dumber having Travis in charge. Maybe I'm being burned for things I've done in the past. Looks like God is getting back at me."

Dan wished he could address this, but right now he felt like God was out to get him, too. Now he understood why Evan left the building with his chin on his chest. Dan was about to have his head on the floor. "Todd, I wish you would let me stay on."

"Wish I could, too. I'll keep in touch."

Dan took his final paycheck and left. He stared at the floor, tracing the patterns of linoleum just as Evan had done. *I don't believe this. I–I've just been fired.* He looked at his paycheck. Only a week's worth. He had his mortgage coming up. His car payment. And he hadn't saved a dime like Pop always taught him to. He'd spent it all. *Okay, don't panic. There has to be other places hiring guides for the upcoming summer. You can get a job.*

Dan tried to calm himself, but all he felt was despair. And questions. And anger toward earring girl and her fancy-pants father. And everything else.

Now he did what he thought he'd never do. He went directly to the competitor's place. Inside was hopping with eager customers shopping and looking to book tours. Travis looked very happy. "Is Chris around?" Dan asked.

"He's real busy. What's the matter with you?"

"I just got fired. So I'm in a lousy mood."

"Now you know what it feels like, huh? C'mon back." Dan's spirits rose as he followed Travis into a back office. It was a much classier place than Todd's, he had to admit. Professional. Even had an espresso machine parked on the counter. Through the window he saw air-conditioned transports. Shiny boats. Dan knew he would love working here. Maybe.

When Travis told Chris that Dan had lost his job, Chris invited Dan to have a seat.

Dan filled him in on all the gory details and then some.

Chris sat there, drumming his fingers on the desk. "Well, as you can imagine, I can't have someone inept handling my boats."

Dan stared. "I wasn't inept. Your employee, Travis, was the

one training me. It was my first day on a boat. He can tell you."

Chris shook his head. "Sorry, can't help you."

"So it's okay to keep an inept guide on your force who can't train worth beans?"

Chris's face darkened. "Travis is an excellent employee. If you don't mind, you can leave my office. There's the door."

Oh man, Dan, what did you do? He took off as fast as he could. Now he walked the streets like a robot. Everyone had smiles on their faces and a lift to their step. The sun was hot. The rocks were flaming red. The sky was blue. And he felt like junk inside. He entered another rafting place and introduced himself. They shook their heads when he asked about employment. So did a third. Dan then spotted a saloon open for business, despite it being 10:00 a.m. Well, why not? He had nothing better to do today.

He ambled in, took a seat right at the bar, and ordered a beer. How could this have happened? Not long ago, everything was going perfectly. And a month ago, Jo had invited him into her apartment of all things! Now this. He downed his beer in several gulps and ordered another.

"Better watch it, guy," said the bartender. "Little early for this."

"I don't care. I just got fired."

He shook his head. "Sorry to hear that."

"You wouldn't be hiring, would you? I'd even bus tables."

"No one is now, I'm afraid. Sorry."

What am I going to do? He intended to bury it all in his beer, but the liquid made him feel worse. It did not deaden the pain but created a lump in his throat. He nearly asked for a third beer when he heard the door open and close. And then he saw her. Jo. Why would Jo be at a saloon of all places on the globe? These places were off-limits to Christian people. It was beneath them. Saloons were only good for lowlifes like himself.

Instead Jo walked over and sat down beside him. If he were not losing his senses now in the beer, mixed with his problems, he would have considered this another miracle of God. But it also made him feel strange, too, knowing Jo's Christianity and her seeing him nurse his troubles over a beer.

"I'll have a root beer," she told the bartender.

"How'd you know I was here?"

"I followed you. Took me a bit to get the nerve to walk in here. This isn't my usual hangout."

"You shouldn't be in here at all," he said shortly.

"Or you either. Look, I knew this was coming. Todd told me about it a few days ago. He likes you a lot, Dan. More than you know. But until this blows over, we felt it best to get you out of the picture."

"So will you go out of business?"

"I hope not. I pray not. But we're already feeling it. Word is out there and our trips are already down. People are canceling trips. Which is why we had to let Evan go, too. We'd hired him just before you."

Despite his own troubles, Dan realized that Jo had troubles of her own.

"I'm sorry this happened," she added.

"I am, too. I gave it all I had. I tried to do the best I could."

"Todd knows that."

"But it wasn't enough to see this through. I mean, to let me go just like that." He snapped his fingers. "I went to see Chris, thinking maybe I could find work at his place. Of course, now he knows what happened."

"Oh, Dan!" she groaned. "Why did you do that? Now it's going to make things worse."

"Because I need the work to pay my bills, Jo!" His voice was louder than he intended, but he didn't care. He wasn't going to be blamed for going to Chris. Or anything else. "I need work. I got bills coming. Man, what a time to lose a job."

"I thought you had savings."

"I used to, but. . ." He refused to tell her how he'd spent it all, everything his father had given him when he left Virginia. Gone to personal things like going out. The Jeep. The house and everything inside it. "I've got bills due. I've got to find something quick."

"C'mon, let's go see if we can find some leads." She downed her root beer and tugged on his hand.

Dan didn't budge. For some reason, Jo's willingness to help rubbed him the wrong way, and he didn't know why. "Look, you don't have to pity me. I can take care of myself. I'll be fine."

"Dan, I'm just trying to help."

"Thanks, but I'll be fine on my own." He managed a lopsided grin before standing and leaving the saloon. He didn't need advice or anyone's help at this stage. He'd made it once in Moab; he'd make it again. But the wall of doubt was rising quicker than his confidence.

eleven

Life on the fast track had suddenly come to a screeching halt, and Dan felt numb by it. For the first time, he watched other rafting companies load up their vehicles with equipment and personnel, but he was not among the ones helping. Or guiding trips. Or setting up camp and leading night stalks with the kids. Despite his best effort, scouring out at least a dozen outfitters, no one wanted to hire him. Word had gotten around about the lawsuit, and somehow they believed he was at fault.

"Can't take the risk," said one owner, his shades hanging from the strap at his neck. He was wearing fancy board shorts and a sleeveless shirt.

"I'm not a risk. Look, you can try me free for a week. If you like what I do, we can make it permanent. I've got a license and everything."

The guy shook his head. "It's all over that you were involved in the act that led to the lawsuit at Red Canyon Adventures. There's no way I can take a chance like that with my company."

Dan couldn't believe it. Now he was branded a work hazard all because he was learning the ropes that first day under Travis's tutelage. Travis had a job and he didn't. How he wanted to trash the guy's name from here to Salt Lake City. The more he thought about it, the angrier he became. The guy who was to blame got off scot-free and even had a good job to boot. Dan was innocent, and yet he was the one with the brand on his neck.

He took the Jeep that day and scouted out the hidden places in and around Moab. But even the interesting rock formations and town hangouts failed to comfort him. No longer did he lead enthusiastic groups down the Colorado, hearing their exclamations along with the thrill of the moment as the rafts bobbed over the rapids. Instead he listened to the anxiety of his heart thumping madly in his chest and the endless questions circulating in his brain, wondering how this could have happened.

To make matters worse, he still felt guilty over the way he'd treated Jo at the saloon. For having had such an interest in her in the past, to cast her away like he did went beyond his comprehension. He should've accepted her advice with open arms. She might've had some ideas about employment. She'd been here much longer than him anyway. And he threw her away like a hunk of scrap. Many times he wanted to call her cell or even knock on the door of her apartment. But instead he sat brooding in his house, looking at his laptop, wondering how much longer he would have these comforts before he must sell things to make ends meet.

Dan sighed. He'd had such wild expectations for a future in Utah from the glossy pictures and attention-grabbing ads. A new home away from the old. Now he considered it all. The old homestead was never like this. Oh, he'd had his brotherly spats with Rob, which amounted more to jealousy than anything. He'd had his times of boredom working the family farm. He poked fun at Mom and Pop who did everything by the Holy Book, so to speak. Here in Moab, he wanted to make a name for himself. To show everyone, the world, himself, God, that he could make it and make it big. Now what did he have to show for it? Zip, zero, zilch.

A knock on the door drew him out of his contemplation.

Surely it couldn't be the employment office with news of a job for him. Maybe Todd was coming to relent and offer him his old job back. He'd even cook if that's what it came down to. Dan opened the door to reveal Jo. Normally an encounter like this should have knocked him off his feet and allowed love to take over. But he looked at her as if she had a sign around her neck saying, *You deserve it. If only you'd kept your big paws off me.*

"Hi, Dan."

"Hey." He made no move to invite her in. Instead he moved to the two deck chairs on the porch and plopped down in one. She followed suit.

"We missed you at game night. All the guys were asking where you were, especially at the Monopoly table. I told them that Todd had to let you go."

Great. Now all of Moab knows. Mr. Big Shot is now The Biggest Loser. And it wasn't because of a weight-loss competition on reality TV—he was a loser in life. "Thanks a bunch."

"Dan, c'mon. You can't do this alone. There are people who care about you. By the way, Brian said to give you this. He saw it on a bulletin board in town." She handed the paper to him.

Dan took it halfheartedly and stared at it. It described an employment opportunity in the sanitation department. "You're kidding, right? Isn't this the same thing as a garbage collector?"

"Dan, it's a job. Moab is pretty short on them these days. You need to take whatever is out there. It's only temporary, just to make ends meet until something else opens up. Or this thing with Todd blows over and business picks up, which we hope it does soon."

Dan perked up at this. Maybe there was a light at the end of this dark tunnel. "You mean Todd might hire me back?"

"I don't know. We're having the case reviewed to see where it stands and where we stand as a company. We probably won't know anything for a while. And I'm sure you're gonna need money soon."

"But there has to be something better than a garbage worker. Hauling trash cans. . .you've got to be kidding."

"You can try and ask around, Dan, but all I've seen is part-time work. And part-time is not going to pay the bills, I'm sure."

Her gaze drifted to his fine ranch house, which among other things had a loan attached to it. He couldn't argue with her. If there was one thing Dan couldn't do, that was default on his loans and have more bad stuff attached to his name, such as a bad credit rating. Besides, this was sure to be temporary. Todd might hire him back at a moment's notice. Or something else would open up. Maybe if he was patient enough, one of Jo's famous miracles from God would pop up. Like the miracle at the RV park when they ran into those girls from the very family he needed to find.

He took out his cell phone and dialed the number on the paper while Jo sat there expectantly. He spoke to the guy in charge. "It's not a job most people will do," the man said, "but it's good pay." Dan noted the details of the job in his brain. He hung up and pocketed the phone.

"Well?"

"They need workers. It looks promising."

Jo jumped to her feet as if he had just been given the word of the day with sunbeams attached. "I just knew it! I know this is God."

He stared. "This is my answer from God, to demote me

from river guide to trash hauler?"

"No, that He provided you with work. It's His provision, Dan, and His blessing, too. If only you don't get too close-minded to see it. "

He felt the defenses rising quickly, like metal barricades. "Let's not go down that road, please. I'm not in the mood for a religious lecture."

"It's not a religious lecture. There is more to life than you or me or anything. You need to see the big picture. Other things are at work here. All this may not be just for you."

"Really. Who else is gonna benefit?"

"There's eternal things. Trials come up in life for a reason. They test us and shape us into the person God wants us to be. And it's not only us who are affected, but others, too."

Dan again felt his irritation on the rise. Jo was trying to be helpful, but her words were more akin to rubbing red desert rock in raw wounds. "Look, I've got some stuff to do. The guy wants to interview me as soon as possible. Guess he needs people to do his dirty work for him." His face scrunched up at the words. "Sorry, bad pun."

"Okay, see you later." She didn't seem put out, but he was definitely putting her out. Or rather putting out her godly ideas that were grating on him, reminding him of his lack of interest in religious things. He thought of dear Mom, picturing her on her knees in his old room, praying for her wayward son. Maybe even praying that something like this would happen in his life. That he would rise to the pinnacle of his career and then hit bottom in a Dumpster along with the rest of the garbage. He wondered how he could ever come out smelling like a rose after all this.

The next afternoon Dan arrived home, newly instated in the trash collecting business as garbage man number five.

There could be worse things in life, he reasoned, like no employment at all. He should be grateful for small things, however small they seemed to be. But he found no comfort. He'd come here to make a living by leading rafting trips. Now he would make his mark on Moab by dealing in their trash.

He flipped open the laptop to find a friend request from Jo. He accepted it. And lo and behold, the chat box popped up.

So how did the interview go? she typed in.

Got the job.

Wow, that's great.

What's so great about collecting trash? Please enlighten me.

I've heard you can tell a lot about people by their trash.

So I'm going to study food wrappers to see what they eat or the magazines they're dumping out. Better than interviewing them to get the inside scoop, I suppose.

I was trying to be funny. I guess I wasn't.

Dan thought about that. No, I guess I didn't think this would happen to me. I had such great expectations about everything.

Sometimes things happen when you don't expect it.

Tell me about it.

The chat box remained empty. He nearly closed it down when another message popped up.

So how about some ice cream when I get off work? You know the old saying, life's short, eat dessert first.

Ice cream. What a novel idea. Dan sighed, wishing he

didn't feel so sour. SURE, WHY NOT? he typed.

OKAY. MEET YOU AT THE SHOP AROUND 6:00.

He closed down communications. Jo really was a special person. And he was realizing more and more how much he didn't deserve her. Oh sure, he once thought himself the perfect male, ready to capture a woman's heart. But Jo was too good for him. Too innocent. He should do the right thing and allow her to find the right man for her life. He certainly wasn't the one.

For the first time, Dan climbed in his Jeep feeling humbled. He wasn't all giddy, flexing biceps, his head held high, looking down on others who were worming their way through life. He thought of Rob then. How he looked with contempt on his brother's life. But Rob had stuck it out on the family farm. He was there helping out while Dan wanted to escape it all for some dumb dream. Dan knew he should have waited to see if this path to Utah was the right one rather than going headlong into something that may have been wrong from the beginning. He got a feeling that he should talk to Brian sometime about this stuff. Maybe let him sift through these thoughts and come up with a solution. But right now Dan punched a number on his cell.

"Hey, Rob? Hey, it's Dan." He sensed the surprise over the phone. "Oh, me? Doing okay, I guess. Just wondering how things were going on the farm." He listened as Rob told him of some minor things happening—machinery that needed fixing and then Pop sick for a time with something like the flu. "Well, glad he's better." Pause. "No, I hadn't seen the weather. I sure hope you get some rain soon. Man, six weeks is a long time without any." Pause. "Yeah, it's dry here, too. Never rains, but that's normal." Rob then talked at length about the girl he'd been seeing, one Dan barely remembered.

Dan saw that he'd arrived at his destination—the ice cream shop. "Hey, I'll have to catch you later. Good talking to you."

Jo walked up to the Jeep.

"Guess what? I just called my brother." He hoped for a pat on the back, a verbal "Good for you" or something. Instead she said nothing. He shrugged and followed her into the shop.

"My treat," Jo added.

"Thanks. That makes me feel like a man." She gave him a look, and he responded with a smile. "I'm not being very funny. Really, I appreciate everything you're doing, Jo. I'm sorry my attitude is so bad. I'm just trying to work things out."

"Yeah," she said absently as if lost in thought. He wondered what spawned the sudden disquiet on her part as they both ordered sundaes. He thought she would be jumping up and down over his family contacts. He stepped back to mentally analyze it. Likely Jo was going through things, too. She must have burdens in her heart. The lawsuit thing wasn't just about him. Her cousin's company was affected. *Get your eyes on someone else for a change, Dan. And that doesn't mean looking at the body. The heart would do fine right about now.*

They wandered over with their sundaes to a corner table, the same table where they ate once before. Maybe they should carve their initials in the tabletop or something. "So how are you doing?" Dan asked. "All we've done is talk about me."

"Oh, I'm fine. But I was glad to hear that the job worked out. Which trash are you picking up, residential or commercial?"

"Residential. I'm one of those happy guys that roll out trash cans to the garbage truck or something to that effect. The manager wasn't too specific on official duties, which is fine with me. But hey, since I didn't do so well guiding a raft, maybe I can learn to drive a truck!" He laughed in spite of himself. "Might as well make the most of every opportunity. Just think. Here I am in the red rocks, the arches, and the glory of the Colorado River, and what am I doing? Basking in the garbage of Moab. Yo, baby."

Jo remained silent, and again Dan chastised himself for being full of it as usual. He simmered down enough to ask, "So are you still doing any trips?"

"We try. Our business is down 50 percent. We get people wandering into the store, too, which helps."

"Boy, I miss that place. And grabbing my daily drink and energy bar. But most of all, I miss the family trips. Taking the kids on night stalks. Remember that one you and I did together? And you taught me how to grill the perfect steak."

"It was a nice trip. You were excellent at making the salad."

"All I really want to do is those raft trips. I'll even make salads. Why I got demoted to garbage detail, I'm not sure. Something has to work out, huh? I mean, like you said, there's got to be a reason for this."

"That's a good way to look at it, Dan." She scraped out the last bit of ice cream coated with fudge.

"You're really quiet today. I hope I'm not lording over you with my mouth."

"No, just thinking. When you said how you called your brother today, it made me think about my brother. I haven't talked to him in ages."

Dan tried not show it, but inside everything suddenly stopped. He recalled then what she'd shared about her past and her older brother who took her in when her parents kicked her out of the house. He decided to go gently. "I thought it would be hard. But I just picked up the cell and called. Rob was real cool about it. Talked nonstop about his girlfriend. I didn't say anything about you, of course, because I know you're not into that. I mean, the girlfriend issue and all. We're just friends."

"Thanks, I appreciate that. I never know where things stand with you. One day we can be having a good friendship; the next, you're making another move."

"You don't have to worry about that. The only move I'll be making is to the garbage truck. I've learned my lesson, I think. Or whatever. I'm not exactly sure what the lesson is in all this. To look before I leap into the Colorado River, maybe? Anyway, I was glad I talked to Rob. Maybe you should try calling your brother. Just to say hi. Can't hurt, and it might help."

He saw something flash in her coffee-colored eyes; a certain glint to them. Then they softened as if she were considering his suggestion. Could it be he'd finally had something to offer that might help Jo? Maybe he wasn't such a bad guy after all. Maybe there were some redeeming factors about him.

"I don't know. We haven't talked in so long. I don't even think he'll recognize my voice."

"Sure he will. You're related, for better or for worse. Well, that's a marriage thing. But you know what I mean. Honestly, I couldn't stand Rob. I thought what he was doing in life amounted to nothing. But he really likes what he does, even if it's harvesting peanuts. And it helps Pop out."

"Well, I didn't leave because I was jealous of my brother. It was for other reasons."

Dan felt the wave of happiness in him come to a screeching halt. Something rose up in him, something he hadn't planned on. "What makes you think I was jealous of Rob? I hated what he did is all."

"Of course you were jealous. I know the sibling rivalry stuff. One parent giving more attention to the other sibling, making you feel inferior, like you can't do anything right. That they will never be happy with what you're doing. You can never please them enough, so you try and please yourself to make up for it."

Dan's knees bobbed back and forth under the table. He felt a sudden chill as if something major had happened. Had he been jealous about his father's feelings for Rob and his attention in the family? Maybe he was trying to hunt down approval to make up for what he thought he lacked on Pop's part. All he knew was that another whammy had just been hurled his way, and he wasn't sure how to handle it. "Okay, fine. But what about you? What do you have to deal with concerning your family?"

"I have plenty to deal with, Dan, but I don't want to get into it. I have others who are helping me in those areas, thanks." She stood to her feet. "Well, I'd better go on home."

"I'll drive you."

"That's okay. I like to walk. See you around."

Dan stared after her, watching her petite form and curvy legs walk to the door of the shop. Her ponytail swished as she opened it and hurried out. He wondered what thoughts lurked beneath that ponytail. Deep thoughts that she couldn't yet share with him. If only he didn't find himself in his own personal storm, he might have been able to offer some wisdom. But he had to get his act together first. Find out what was holding him back from being available for Jo and from having her trust him with her personal struggles. He thought he knew. . .but at that moment, the God issue still scared him. *I'm not ready to make that step. Yet. . .*

twelve

The first week on the job seemed to last forever. Instead of the feel of the river and pleasant water cooling him off, Dan sweated buckets while his flesh fried in the hot sun. Not to mention what garbage did in the heat. His nose would never be the same after smelling things souring and decaying. Dragging another huge garbage can toward the back of the truck, Dan decided nothing could be worse than this. He wanted to quit after day two, but when he found his bank account down to nothing, he knew he had no choice. His concern mounted over how he would make ends meet. As it was, he wondered how he would get the money to make the payments until the first paycheck rolled in. The money from Todd paid a few bills, but now he had nothing.

Dan sighed, taking a break to guzzle water out of a cooler tucked in the cab of the truck. The driver, Charles, who'd been at this stuff for years, he said, pointed to the road.

"Get going, Dan. We're already behind schedule."

"C'mon, I need a break," Dan groaned.

"You told me you needed this job. So you'd better keep hauling cans, or you'll be out of a job real quick."

Dan bit back a retort and walked down the road to roll over the next container. He stopped when he saw two people on the front porch. A man and a woman, both wearing swimsuits, sat in lounge chairs opposite each other. They then turned and looked at him. He thought he heard one of them laugh but couldn't tell. He averted his gaze and rolled the can along the street toward the open end of the truck where the odor nearly knocked his dirty sandals off his feet.

"Hey, Dan!" a voice called out.

He whirled, wondering if he'd actually heard his name or if the garbage was calling to him. The guy bounded down the driveway, dressed in board shorts and wearing shades. Dan thought about his expensive shades and decided he ought to put them on Craigslist to help pay the electric bill.

"What are you doing, man?" Travis stood before him, wearing a grin.

"I'm having fun," Dan said sourly. "Looks like you're having fun, too. The real kind."

"It's my day off." He looked at Dan, the garbage can, and then the truck. "You're kidding. You're working with the sanitation department now?"

"Why not? It's a living. Besides, I hear you can learn all kinds of things about people from their trash." He opened the lid to the can. "Anything I should know about you in here? I suppose it's all legal, too."

The smile disappeared from his face for only a moment before a grin returned. "Wow, I really thought Todd would hire you back. He liked what you did for the company. Kind of got to me a couple of times, but hey, having him fire me actually saved me. Got my job with Chris, and now I'm secure."

He didn't say it, but Dan could finish Travis's thought pattern. *You got yourself let go when no one was hiring. Better you than me.* "Well, things tend to work out in the end," Dan added in a burst of faith.

Travis swiped his sandal across the ground, stirring up red dust. "Too bad it happened. Guess if Todd had kept his nose out of other people's business, he wouldn't be in the mess he's in. He got what was coming to him."

"Hey Dan, get back to work!" Charles called from the driver's window. "You're putting us way behind schedule!"

"You'd better get back to your garbage detail, Dan. Don't want to keep the cans waiting."

The snicker grated on him more than a cheese grater rubbing against his skin. He felt anger burn in him as well as questions. Like what Travis said about Todd. He knew the company Travis worked for had problems with Todd, especially over the salmonella incident. He had to wonder if there was some correlation between that and the current lawsuit.

"You'd better quit with the socializing, kid," Charles said, scratching his head beneath his hat. "That's the problem with hiring you young kids. You don't know what hard work means."

"I've known plenty of hard work in my life," Dan retorted. "I worked my old man's peanut field for years, since I was seven years old."

"Then why are you here and not back there helping him out? That kind of thing usually stays in the family."

"I–I've got a brother who seems to know it all." His voice faded away as he went to roll over another can. Why was he here anyway? That was a good question. Why had he sacrificed the good life with the family—everything he needed, like shelter, food, clothes, peace—for this place? Sure it had been the lure of the river. The glory of rafting. The feel of being a big shot behind the paddle. But what did it bring him now? And especially this mess of the lawsuit and maybe even a rival company out to bury Todd in the red Utah dust.

When they finally finished the route for the day, Dan decided to give Jo a call and tell her what he'd learned from

Travis. Or what he thought he might have learned. The cell rang, but she didn't answer. He left her a message on voice mail. He wished he had time to go over to the store, but he hadn't set foot there since the day he was let go. Too many painful memories and probably leftover anger with Todd as well, though now it seemed to have lessened. In fact, he felt sorry for the guy who had enemies out to get him. Dan sure didn't want to be in that kind of predicament, though he didn't relish his current predicament either.

Right now he had other things to worry about, like his finances. He decided to be bold and ask his boss for an advance on his pay. He had bills nearly overdue, like his cell phone and the electric bill. He had to get his hands on some money, and another week without income wouldn't cut it.

Dan ventured inside the building, stood before the wooden door for a few moments to gather his courage, then knocked.

"What do you want?" the boss called out. "I'm on the phone."

Oh, man. "It's Dan Mallory. I. . .uh, I need to talk to you about something, Mr. O'Donnell."

He heard the man talking loud and fast, discussing dinner plans and the drink he wanted after work. The phone slammed. "All right, come in."

The door creaked open to reveal the man lighting up a cigarette. The office was cluttered with all kinds of things Dan couldn't begin to sort out in his beleaguered mind. Most of it probably deserved to be part of the trash they hauled. "Sir, I have a question. I'm, well, I'm running short on cash right now, having switched jobs and all. I was wondering if I could get an advance on my paycheck."

"I pay on the fifteenth of the month," the man stated, blowing out a puff of smoke.

Dan tried not to sneeze as the smoke tickled his nose, and

his throat turned raw. "I know it's unusual, but I've got some bills due right now and—"

"Gotta budget, kid. That's what I keep telling my eighteen-year-old who goes and spends his cash like its water. Gotta save. And you get paid on the fifteenth. That's that."

He felt a chill descend on him despite the stuffiness inside the office. "Sir, I—"

"Look, go have a bake sale. Wash cars. But that's how I run things here. I don't give handouts. You get paid when you work and on my schedule." The man's glare showed Dan the conversation had ended.

Dan meekly closed the door. In his mind he saw the bills lining the counter at home, all with ominous due dates on them, outlined in red. He was going to be late paying them, and even three weeks late on some. What was he going to do?

He thought then of people he could ask for a loan. Maybe someone at church, but he couldn't bring himself to do that. He could never ask Pop either. As it was, he'd taken his inheritance and spent it all. Jo didn't have any, especially with the way business had dropped off in recent weeks. She was surely hurting financially, too.

He strode outside and looked around until his gaze rested on his Jeep. There was only one thing he could do—take Mr. O'Donnell's advice. He needed money, and he needed it now. Selling other things in classifieds would take time. He got in and drove to a used car lot. From the dust the Jeep had been purchased, and now it would return to the red dust of a used car lot in Moab.

An hour later, he had lost another two thousand dollars with the trade-in, but at least he had the cash to pay the bills. But none of this really helped. He was sinking into the mud, or rather, the dust, as it was too dry around here for anything else. He was being swallowed up by things he couldn't control. As he walked along, he began to cough. He smelled garbage. He saw a few garbage cans still sitting by the curb, and he shuddered. What had he become? What had his decisions led him to? They were supposed to lead him to Shangri-La, but instead, they led him to the bowels of life and the stench to match.

As he walked along staring at the red ground, he thought of green fields. The smell of the rich earth. The pleasant breeze. The joy of a harvest. He was back in Virginia at Pop's peanut fields. Pop was coming home that day after seeing the first harvest. He was there to divvy up the money with Dan and Rob after going to the bank. And Mom had ordered an extra large pizza to celebrate. His favorite, too. A meatza with everything on it.

Now Dan reluctantly passed Zack's and their pizza, along with the Moab Diner. There was no money for pizza or a taco supreme but enough for boxes of mac and cheese, which he bought at the store the other day. His legs ached as he walked, and he realized he'd been on his feet all day. Charles complained he should have work boots and not the fancy river sandals. And it was a long walk from his place of work to home. A very long walk. Several miles at least, or it felt like it.

Now he realized what Jo went through. She had no vehicle and walked everywhere. She lived a life of humble means. He paused to check his cell, which had remained silent all day. She'd still not returned his call, which was strange. She'd vanished like everyone else, no longer interested in keeping company with a garbage collector. And he couldn't blame her.

He continued to ponder it all when he noticed a figure in the distance. He stopped short, recognizing the familiar brown shorts, the hair caught up in a ponytail, and a purse in the shape of a small backpack. It was Jo, and she was laughing at something, or rather, with someone. And it wasn't the fact of her smiling face but who she was smiling at. Some guy he'd never seen before. Tall. Suntanned. Clad in shorts and a polo shirt. The guy said something. She laughed again and waved her hand. They began walking. Dan knew he had no business following them, but he did anyway. They soon headed into Jo and Dan's private haven, of all places in Moab. The ice cream shop.

Dan stopped dead in his tracks. Peering into the window, he saw them order his and Jo's favorite treat, two sundaes. He licked his dry lips, wishing he were feeling the cold creaminess running down his throat. But soon the feeling became replaced by anger. Frustration. Bitterness. Pain. And the feeling of a very dry mouth. Jo had found someone with the right look, driving the right car, who had all the right stuff and a wallet loaded with cash. Now that Dan was in the garbage business, she had linked arms with someone else.

He whirled and continued the long walk back home. But even the word *home* didn't feel right. This place was not home anymore. He'd tried to make Moab a home. He'd given it his all, his soul even, to make this place his. But Jo had warned him long ago that he was only bringing his problems with him. That no matter how far he strayed from Virginia, all the things he thought he left behind still remained. His dissatisfaction with life. His search for true meaning. What he was supposed to do. How he was supposed to live.

Dan finally arrived home an hour later, his feet aching, dirty, and blistered, vowing to find himself a clunker somewhere if there was any money left from paying the bills. He had several boxes of mac and cheese in the otherwise bare cupboard and made himself a large potful. He then went to check in on the social network and saw a friend request from Rob, along with a note:

> *Hey, bro. Glad we talked. I'm thinking of scrounging together some money and coming out to see what you do there in Moab with the rafting and all. Let me know when would be a good week. Maybe you can get me a good deal on a rafting trip.*

Dan stared. Rob wanted to come out here and see what he did? He could see it now. The snickering Travis offered today would pale by comparison. He'd hear Rob's laughter and "I told you so" and "You never had it so good in Virginia," and other assorted sayings to make him feel lower than the landfill site. He accepted Rob's friend request but did not answer him right away. Instead he sat back to think about a response. If he didn't answer, Rob might book a flight immediately. Whether he said something now or later, Rob would eventually find out he was a simple trash collector. If only there was some way he could find another job in a rafting company somewhere. He straightened. Maybe Jo and Todd would let him take a raft for one day. He could pretend to be a part of the company. Show off his stuff to Rob and then send him on his way.

Instead he slumped down in the chair. Like that was the solution, pretending everything was fine and dandy when it wasn't. Living a lie, which is what he'd been doing for eighteen months. He took up the laptop and composed a message.

> *Hey, Rob. Sorry, but now's not a good time for a visit. Things haven't worked out right with the rafting*

company, and I was let go. So I won't be able to take you up on a rafting trip right now.

He conveniently left out the part about the lawsuit and his new job. Rob didn't need to know the particulars. He read it over and hit the ENTER key. At least he was able to confess that he was no longer working for Red Canyon Adventures.

Rob was online, for a message came back within a few minutes.

Sorry to hear about your situation. It's been tough here, too, and with the drought, Pop is looking at a major loss. I'm already looking for another job.

With these words, Dan sensed a change in his attitude. The feelings of anger and jealousy and the sibling rivalry that always reared its ugly head when they came together began to fade. Now he was seeing a brother. Someone who cared. Someone who wanted to share in life's difficulties. And he felt something else, too. Shame on his part that he wasn't there to help Mom and Pop in their time of need. That while they were hurting, he was having his own pity party in the red clay. He'd not even spoken to them since Christmas, he thought. He couldn't remember the last time. It was amazing to see how things that once tore at him now opened his heart. Like his family.

Dan leaned back against the chair, thinking about him and Rob in a tent in the backyard, tossing peanut shells at each other. He was adrift then in memory, to water floats down the James River, a lesson with Pop behind the wheel of the tractor and the car, a Mother's Day brunch he and Rob fixed for Mom. . .

A knock came on the door. Dan jumped and looked at the time. He'd been dozing for a half hour, his head on the table beside his laptop. He came groggily to his feet, swaying. It was already 7:00 p.m.

A knock came again.

He stumbled forward, wiping his face, and opened the door. Jo stood there with the aroma of Chinese food wafting in the air. "Hi, Dan."

He stared from the top of her head to the leather sandals on her feet. "What are you doing here?"

She stepped back. "Well, hi to you, too. What kind of a greeting is that?"

"Sorry about that." He stepped aside.

She walked in and went to the kitchen table where the bills were spread out. "Paying your bills?"

"Yeah," he said, plunking down into a chair. He closed up the laptop and stowed it away.

"Don't worry. It will get better. How's the job?"

"Nice and smelly." He inhaled the Chinese food as she opened the little white cartons to reveal shrimp lo mein, moo goo gai pan, rice, and egg rolls. "I don't have a lot of money. . . ," he began.

"My treat. I wasn't in the mood to eat alone."

"I didn't think you were alone," he added a bit stiffly, flying to his feet to retrieve some plates and forks. At once the vision of her with the guy at the ice cream store took over.

"What's that supposed to mean?"

Dan shrugged. "I saw you at our hangout—the ice cream shop today."

Jo stared, puzzled, until her eyes widened. "Oh, you mean you saw Neil and me?"

"Sure, you and Neil. Is he the new guy Todd hired?"

"What? Of course not. He's Brian's brother."

Great. Brian had a holier-than-thou brother. And now the holy brother had his holy hooks in Jo. So much for that. Easy come—well, it wasn't easy by any means—easy go.

"I was showing him around town. And he was hot, so we went for ice cream." Her head tipped to one side. "Dan? Do you have a problem?"

I have multiple problems. I want you to be my girlfriend, but I can't begin to keep you with the kind of life I'm leading right now. And now a holy brother comes to town, probably with lots of cash to treat you right, standing on a good, solid foundation, leaving me out and him in. Dan looked at the Chinese food that was slowly starting to cool, but nothing came out of his mouth.

"Neil is a lawyer, Dan," she explained to his unspoken inquiry. "He's going to help Todd look over our situation. He actually flew in to be with Brian, and it so happened he had some spare time to help out our company." She paused then added, "Before he flies back home to his family in Texas."

"His family lives in Texas?" Dan repeated in a high-pitched voice.

"His wife and two daughters. Yes, he's married, so you can relax." And suddenly she was grinning as if enjoying this little game.

If Dan wasn't so famished and Jo wasn't who she was, he would have taken her in his arms right then and planted a big fat kiss on her juicy red lips. Instead he ate his egg roll before commenting. "So you think it's funny to lead me on like that?"

"It was kind of neat watching you squirm. I'll have to admit, I've never had a guy do that."

"Sure you have. That James guy."

"Are you kidding? He didn't care about me. He had his drug habit. It's kind of nice, actually, to have a guy jealous.

Makes me feel wanted." She ended it with a giggle before tasting her moo goo gai pan.

He would have enjoyed this time more if not for the present circumstances of poverty and trash collecting and everything else grotesque. And feeling as if he could never match up to Jo's expectations. Yet she did come by with a great Chinese dinner, which he now took over to the microwave to reheat. He then volunteered to heat up hers as well. When they sat down, something passed between them. What was it about sharing meals that brought about a certain bonding?

He shared then about his meeting with Travis earlier and his suspicions.

"I'm not going to worry about it. Trying to make a connection between the two scenarios of Todd and Chris will only make things worse. I'm just glad Neil's here. It shows God is on our side. We can be victorious through Him." She cast him a look when he stayed silent. "Yes?"

"I'm just thinking how much I feel like a loser right now. Cool is out and poor is in. Maybe you'd do better to hang out with the lawyer types. I know this Neil guy is married, but you know what I mean. I'm sure there's plenty to choose from, or at least from the rafting guys in Moab."

"Dan, c'mon. You're in some tough times right now, sure. Lots of people are in your situation. That doesn't make you any less of a quality human being, despite other flawed areas."

"Aha, I knew we would get into it. What flawed areas in particular are you referring to?"

"Well, like your Christian walk. Before you can do anything else in life, you really need to see where you stand with God and what He is in your life. If you want to talk to Brian about it, I'm sure he would be glad to help."

Dan paused to consider her words. He admitted he did murmur a prayer or two these days. He had no choice, with his ever-shrinking wallet and ever-increasing bills. But then there were the feelings of anger over Travis. The disgust at his present job. Wondering if God was saying from the great throne room of heaven, "You deserve it all, Dan, you poor man. Leaving your family in the peanut field to come here to seek your fortune. And for what? Look at what's left."

"I can see you're thinking about it," Jo added.

"I'm trying to sort things out, yeah. But religion is something I need to do on my own schedule. No one else's, you know what I mean?"

"The only religion you need is what lies between the covers of a Bible. In there is everything for salvation and the true meaning of life. Our purpose for existing."

Jo's words stayed with Dan long after she said good night. He had a Bible somewhere, the one he used as a prop the night he went to Jo's apartment, seeking answers. But now he really needed those answers. Maybe it would do him good to look at the Bible and see what it had to say. Something different might come out of an exercise like that.

thirteen

Jo always believed there was more to life than what meets the eye. God did not make mistakes. Despite everything that had happened with Dan, the job, Todd, her life, God knew it all. He knew what would happen, which people would be involved, and the outcome. And right now, Jo's thoughts and prayers were centered on a particular outcome. She wanted to see good come of all that was happening, even if Dan couldn't see the good right now. And sometimes she struck gold with seeing it, too. Now was the time for faith to take over and trust for a godly outcome.

Not a day would go by when Jo wasn't thinking about Dan or praying for him. At first she found him rather obnoxious. A bit full of himself and his own desires in life. But these days she was seeing him in a new light. He'd been handed a raw deal, finding himself saddled with a job he disliked and barely able to make ends meet. But good could come of something like that. The situation could move him to do some soul-searching where the things of God were concerned and place him at a point where God could reach him.

Jo thought about it as she sat before the silent cash register. With their rafting business slowed to a crawl because of the lawsuit, just a few visitors came by to look at the leftover merchandise. Only a few employees remained, with barely enough to cover the rafting trips they did conduct. When they didn't have the personnel to do extra trips, Jo asked the visitors for their information so they could be alerted when the trips became available. She hoped they would soon be able to hire employees back, especially Dan.

At that moment a family of four came strolling in with smiles on their faces. The kids immediately headed for the aquatic toys while Dad and Mom came up to speak with Jo. "We were here last year for the family rafting trip, and we just had to do it again with your guide named Dan. It was a marvelous time, and the kids loved it."

Jo sighed. Another family requesting Dan's presence. "I'm sorry, but he no longer works here."

Mom and Dad stared at each other in surprise. "Oh no," Mom groaned. "The kids asked for him."

"This is the only trip the kids wanted to do," the dad explained. "They just loved Dan. He took them on that night hike or something by the river. They said that was their favorite part. He's a natural at it."

Jo smiled and offered them another trip with a different guide, which they reluctantly accepted. The kids then came over with their selections—aquatic glasses and bubbles. Jo liked seeing the cash register open with business, but even more than that, she liked what the mom and dad had to say about Dan. With every word they spoke, Jo sensed something welling up in her heart. *Dan would make a great dad*, she mused before straightening in her seat. He would make a great dad? *That means he has to be a husband.* Jo shook her head, just as Todd walked in.

"What's the matter?" he asked.

"Another family came in here wanting a trip with Dan. They said he was the best." She squinted as she looked at Todd. "Isn't there any chance we can hire him back? He's miserable as a garbage collector."

"Not until things have cleared up. I can't take the chance."

"I'm not asking, I'm pleading. People love him. The kids think he's the greatest. He's a hard worker, Todd."

"I know he's a hard worker."

"And he had nothing to do with the lawsuit."

"I know that, too. I'm just trying to figure out what to do. We're running into trouble financially as it is. I'm not sure how we can keep our head above water."

"Todd, if you advertise this as a family-oriented rafting company, with overnight trips and night stalks to complement it, you're going to generate more business."

"I can't just do that. I do need some high-level trips like Cataract Canyon for the college crowd."

"But I think we should gear this company toward the family. Like those water parks and other places that are family friendly. We could get some playground equipment, too."

"Oh, Jolene, honestly." He rolled his eyes, but a smile remained on his face.

"I'm just thinking out loud. But one thing you really need to consider is Dan. It's a waste having him deal in Moab's trash. He's got talent that our company can use."

"Yeah, and he knows it, too."

"But he's going through a lot right now. A complete spiritual makeover is in full progress, I'd say."

Todd's eyebrow rose. "I'm sure you've had a hand in that department."

"I've shared about God, if that's what you mean. Same as I'd do with you, if you wouldn't give me the I-can't-listen-to-that-kind-of-thing routine."

"Believe me, Jolene, I've done my share of thinking these past few weeks. It was an answer to prayer when your youth pastor's brother came by, willing to help me with the lawsuit." He paused. "From what Neil is saying, he believes he can get the case dropped due to insufficient evidence. He plans on contacting the lawyer of the insurance company to see if the details can be worked out to our benefit."

"Wow, that's great!" She stood and gave him a hug.

"Guess you have it in good with that church of yours and the Man upstairs."

Jo sighed and shook her head. "Man upstairs, ha. He's also downstairs and all around. And He cares, Todd."

Todd took off before she could say any more. Hope was rekindled with Todd's announcement about the lawsuit. Hope was also growing to a roaring blaze where Dan was concerned. Especially on the heels of the family visit to the shop, with the mom and dad praising his ability. She ought to go see him and tell him. Give him something positive to gnaw on. Hope deferred makes the heart sick. But in this case, hope could bring health and healing to a man's troubled heart. And Jo couldn't wait to give the remedy.

❧

Jo drove up to Dan's house in Todd's car. The place appeared quiet to her, even melancholic in a way. The windows were dark. Not a flower could be seen anywhere, though guys rarely had flowers anyway. A cloud of depression seemed to hang over the place. How she wished she'd stopped and bought a basket of flowers to hang on his porch. Flowers to Jo symbolized hope. She didn't see many flowers in Moab except for those that came out in spring, struggling to find life in Utah's red soil. But the markets still carried baskets of flowers that people often displayed in front of their homes.

Jo backed out of the driveway with an idea in mind. She hastened for the nearest market and wasted no time buying a basket. Driving back, she saw a figure marching down the sidewalk, head held high. She pushed down the button of the window, receiving a blast of hot air. "Hi, Dan. Want a lift?"

"Hey. Guess I'm getting used to this walking routine, even though I need to get myself a car. Know any cheap ones?"

"C'mon, hop in. I have something for your home, so I'm headed that way."

"I hope it's a check." He laughed shortly and entered the passenger seat. "So what do you have?"

"You'll see. How was work?"

"The usual. Can't you smell it?"

She shook her head. "Maybe. I smell outdoors stuff and a guy whose deodorant is wearing off. But I've worked around Todd now for a long time. You get used to guy smells in the great outdoors." Jo smiled, hearing Dan laugh a bit as he settled in the seat, adjusting the vents so that the air-conditioning blew on his face.

"This feels so good. I've decided that I may never go back to walking. You can pick me up and drive me home every day if you want."

"I'm not sure how Todd will react to his vehicle becoming the Moab taxicab."

"I was kidding. But it's easy to get spoiled. Probably why I'm in the mess I'm in. I was too spoiled. I've been thinking it over. God had to knock me over somehow. And it might as well be with a garbage truck. I've heard how people make idols out of their personal stuff and how God ends up taking it all away."

"Well, sometimes He does. But sometimes it's just the natural course of things. The point is, He can still work through them." She arrived at his home and opened the side door to retrieve the planter. Dan stood beside her, staring at it.

"You're kidding, right? You're turning my masculine bachelor pad into a *Gone with the Wind* plantation home?"

"I don't know, but the house looked kind of sad to me. Flowers mean there's life. You have to admit that plants can really speak things."

"I used to make fun of Pop's peanut plants. The only thing they spoke to me was a dull and dreary life. But I'm thinking more and more that I would like to see them again. The folks, that is."

"You should go back for a visit."

His face colored. He scraped his sandal along the ground. "I don't think I could do that."

"Why not?"

"I don't know. I acted like the Clyde part of Bonnie and Clyde when I took the money and ran. I lost all of Pop's inheritance. I don't think it would be a warm reception."

Jo took the planter and, to her delight, found a hook ready and available on the front porch. She watered the pot from the outside spigot, hooked it up, then stepped back for a view. "There. Perfect. One big happy home."

"Made by the happy homemaker, which I most definitely am not. I'd invite you in, Jo, but the house is hotter than that place no one wants to go to, and I have nothing in the fridge."

"Why is it hot in your house?" She then thought about it and nodded. "You really are living the life of a vagabond."

"I'm barely keeping the house. I've already missed a mortgage payment. I have to make the next or I'm going to be experiencing camping in a whole new way."

"Okay, then. Let's go somewhere. What about Arches?"

Dan stepped back. "Arches? I'm surprised."

"I love that place. Why not?"

"I don't know. Maybe because I burned you there. Took advantage of a situation that I shouldn't have."

"I'm not in the habit of keeping count of it all. You said

you were sorry, didn't you?"

"Yeah, but. . ."

From the look on his face, she didn't think he was that sorry for what happened on their hike to Delicate Arch. And she had to admit, at this point, she wasn't sorry either. "Arches would be good," she decided. "We'll stop at the market for fried chicken and drinks. My treat."

"You're gonna spoil me if you keep this up. The only time I don't eat mac and cheese is when you stop by with food."

What else does a wife do? . . . Oops. There it was again! The husband and wife angle. How could she be thinking that?

The errands for food didn't take long. Dan kept the bag of chicken on his lap, inhaling the aroma as if it were the best thing on earth to him. Jo encouraged him to go ahead and eat a piece if he wanted, but Dan shook his head, vowing to show restraint until they arrived at their destination. Within the hour they were at the Windows section of Arches and spread their picnic near the North and South Window formations.

"They look like a pair of humungous eyes staring at us," Dan commented, munching down his chicken and biscuits as though he had not tasted food in a long time.

"They are windows made by God. Look through them, and what do you see?"

Dan paused, and to Jo's surprise, stood to his feet. She sat there, watching him head up the trail toward the open archway that overlooked the rugged Utah landscape. He returned and sat down on the bench beside Jo. "The view looks cool, that's for sure. It's better up there. Back in Moab, all I see are my problems. Here I can see things in a whole new way. The problems don't seem as big anymore."

"That's why I like it here. If we see those rocks up close and personal, they're just rocks. But from a distance, they form a pretty setting. Just like we're seeing things we've done under our own microscope. But from afar, God sees our mistakes as something He can redeem for His glory."

Dan smirked. "I'm not sure how He can take a life like mine and make it into something cool like an arch."

"He already is. You said how you're seeing God in a different light. And maybe if you go home to Virginia and patch things up. . ."

He picked up a small rock and tossed it. "Maybe. I don't know. I've lived my life the way I wanted. Or thought I wanted. But the idea that now I should ask God's opinion seems kind of strange. What if He calls down from heaven, ignites that bush over there on fire, and says, 'Get thee out of this land of Utah and back to where you belong'?"

"Well, He might. But I think He really wants to know if you're ready to listen and willing to trust Him with your life. I mean, Dan, you've been trusting in your own way of doing things for a lot of years. Not to speak against the mistakes, because I've made a ton myself. But do you think you've done a good job with your life?"

"As a boss of my own identity, hardly."

"Then why not let the true Boss of heaven and earth give your life a try? You certainly don't have anything to lose, and maybe a whole lot to gain."

He tossed another rock. "It would sure make Pop and Mom proud."

"Don't worry about that. Think of what it will do for you, personally." She pointed at the huge round arches of solid stone before them. "Look through God's eyes and not yours. And you're going to find a whole new view on life, guaranteed."

Dan got quiet then, which was unusual for him. The stillness persisted as the sun began to disappear below the horizon. Jo packed up the dinner. She had to return Todd's car before it got too late. As she headed back for the car, she felt a hand on her arm, drawing her to a stop. "Hey, Jo?"

"Yeah, Dan?"

"Don't worry, I won't take advantage of the sunset again. But I do want to tell you that you're something else. I mean, I always knew people cared about me. Like Mom and Pop. I never really appreciated them until now, when I see everything you've done for me these past few weeks. Thanks."

"Sure, Dan." She smiled, spawning a similar smile on his face. They began drifting back to the car. Her arm still tingled under the touch of his hand. She thought that a kiss beneath the setting sun would be nice. When they were both ready for it, that is. And it might be coming sooner than she expected if they could work out the snags of life that remained. But at least she found in Dan a listening ear, more so than ever before. Even if the sun was setting right now, a new dawn may be rising.

❧

"Well, Jo, thanks again for everything," he said, exiting Todd's car at his house. "They talk of heroes rescuing damsels in distress, but it's interesting and humbling to have the damsel rescue the hero."

"Dan, believe me, you're doing your fair share of rescuing, too. See you soon."

Jo thought on her comment as she drove back to Todd's place. All this talk of reconciliation made her reconsider her own life. Her brother, Ross, for example. Everything he'd done for her, which she threw away when he challenged her to make things right. And then her parents in New York, with whom she'd had no real relationship for many years. Yes, Dan might need to make amends with his family, but so did she.

fourteen

If only Dan could believe in Jo's statement. That he was somehow rescuing her with his situation. How he could possibly be doing such a thing, he had no idea. But the thought continued to pester him as he went about his work after a promising weekend filled with interesting conversation and deep thoughts.

Something must have changed up there in Arches, because today he felt more energized. Charles wasn't grumpy either, and in fact, praised Dan for his quick work. "You taking pep pills or something?" the older man finally asked when Dan came jogging up with a can.

"No. Just want to do what I'm supposed to and give it all I have."

The man's eyebrows formed a perfect arch. "Been a long time since I've heard a young person say those things. I hear them say all kinds of stuff and never mean a word of it. But you seem to mean it today."

"I had a good day yesterday."

"Aha. Bet there was a girl in it, huh?"

Dan paused. "Well, yeah, I was with a friend of mine. We went to Arches and hung out. Got to talking and all. Did you know there are arches up there that look like huge eyes staring at you?"

Charles chuckled. "I haven't been there since I was a young man."

"You need to go back. It's great. I'd take you, but I had to sell my Jeep to pay the bills."

Charles stared at him. When Dan entered the cab after finishing with the cans on the street, instead of roaring off to the next neighborhood, Charles sat back and stared at him. "You know what, Dan? You're gonna be all right. And you're gonna go far."

For the first time in a long time, Dan sat dumbfounded. It was hot in the cab, and the sweat was rolling off his forehead, nearly blinding his vision. But he didn't move a muscle. Maybe because he couldn't believe what the man had just said.

"I see you don't believe me. You know why I say it? Because I've been there. I was young like you, you know. A dumb hotshot. Came here seeking my future. And ended up in the garbage business. Which is fine. I don't mind it. I meet interesting people. It pays the bills. But I think, too, about what I could've become and what I had lost. And I don't want you ending up like me. You have a lot going for you. You told me you left your father's farm to come here, right?"

Dan had a difficult time answering; his mouth was so dry. "Yeah."

"You need to start by going back and making things right. No matter what happened or what others have done, it's the right thing to do. Begin where you left off and go from there."

Dan looked off into the distance and the row of garbage cans waiting in expectation for them on the next street. "I don't know if I can. I wasted a lot of things. Money. Life. Choices. And I kind of ran out on the folks."

"It's not too late. When you think it's too late is when the hope is gone, and then you've got nothing to fall back on. But that isn't so in your case. You're young. Don't end up like me, stuck behind this wheel. Don't even end up on a boat either, going nowhere fast. Find out what you're supposed to do in life. But no matter what, don't leave your loved ones out of it. They need you, and you need them."

Dan snickered. "I never thought I was getting anywhere working in a peanut field. But maybe I was only looking at it from one point of view."

"Did you have money? A place to live? Good food? People who loved you?"

"Yeah, everything." He stared out the window to see the heat reflecting off the pavement.

Charles put the truck in gear. It groaned and hissed to the next street. Dan opened the door. When he did, he felt like he was ready to open a new door to life, one he never thought he would open again. Taking hold of another garbage can, he thought about his big getaway plans. He'd gotten away, sure. And learned a heap. Maybe to ready himself for a bigger plan. Something he couldn't have done elsewhere. But what the plan could be, he wasn't entirely sure.

"Just remember what I said," Charles said when he returned. "And know you've got God watching over you. He cares big-time. He's just waitin' for you to make your move and stop saying no to everything and everyone around you."

At the end of the day, Charles and he were buddies. Or rather mentor and mentoree. Charles gave him a smile and a firm pat on the back. Dan soaked it in as he walked home, whistling. He didn't have all the answers, but he was looking at peace for the first time in his life. And Jo had been right about making God the big part of it all. Not in words, a church building, even Mom and her apple pie. But making God personal. Real. Before he handled anything else in life. *I need that*, he thought as he walked along. *I don't want the stained-glass window God. Or the leather book with pages written about God. But the real honest to goodness Person. God, make Yourself real to me. The real deal. Let me say yes.*

"Hey, Dan!"

Dan whirled to see a smiling face peering at him from a car window. It was Brian, the minister from Jo's church. "Need a lift?"

Dan thought of declining, but instead pounced on it and occupied the passenger seat. The air-conditioning felt good. Brian gave him another smile and asked about work.

"It's a living."

He laughed. "Yeah, we need to be happy for any kind of work these days. I'm hearing more and more how people are being laid off. Have to keep a thankful heart, even if the job may be different than we planned." He pulled into a convenience store. "Gotta make a quick stop. I'll leave the engine running."

Dan drummed on the dashboard, letting the cold air blow on his face. It felt refreshing on his hot and dried-out flesh. When Brian returned, he carried two huge slushies and handed one to Dan. "These are great when it's hot out."

Dan stared. "Well, I don't have—"

"Hey, it's on me."

Dan took it slowly, unsure of what to think or say, until the words of his prayer came back to him. *God, make Yourself real to me.* Was God doing just that by presenting him with Brian's friendship and a slushie?

Brian headed onto Main Street, talking about the game night and hoping Dan would come back soon. "We miss you. Monopoly hasn't been the same."

Dan smirked. "Yeah, it was a good time. But I think now I kind of need to start showing up earlier. For the testimonies and all." He looked at his slushie cup, thinking about the testimony in the cold cup he held in his hands. Of God's love and care.

"Hearing testimonies is a good thing. They stir up our faith, especially if it's been cold for a while. Faith can get buried by all kinds of things. But when you stir it up and make it come alive, you realize then that God is love, too. And He becomes real to us."

"Wow, that's just what I've been asking for. That God would be real to me."

"Then let's agree on that together."

Brian prayed a prayer that reached deep into Dan's soul, stirring his faith to life. After it was over, Brian asked if he'd heard about the rafting company and the lawsuit.

"I haven't heard anything yet."

"Might want to head over there sometime soon. I think you'll be surprised."

Dan looked at him, but Brian said nothing more. When Brian pulled into the driveway, Dan invited him in, but he said he had to pick up his kids from soccer practice. "Keep your chin up, Dan. With God in the picture, it can only get better."

It's already getting better, he thought, looking at his empty slushie cup. *Much better than before.* A thirst-quenching, life-giving slushie given to him by a guy who cared. From a guy who had made God commander in chief of his life, but a guy who also showed him how real God could be.

Just then his cell phone played a tune. He could barely make out Jo as her words rushed forth. Something about the rafting company, the lawsuit, and a job. He couldn't quite comprehend it all. Finally, she said she was coming right over and bringing a pizza.

Slushies. Pizza. Charles patting him on the back. He was overwhelmed, so much so that a tear sprang into his eye.

He went into the house to straighten up the few sticks of furniture that remained. The wall was bare—he'd sold the plasma TV. He'd sold his laptop, too, and had taken to going to the library for any computer needs. But the bills had finally been paid, and he'd managed to keep the house. He was living a humble life with all the clutter out of the way. Maybe once he had his act together, he could handle some of the stuff again. But without it, he was seeing and hearing so much better.

A knock came about a half hour later. Jo stood there, her face beaming like the sunrise, holding a huge pizza box. "Dan, we are celebrating!"

Behind her stood Todd along with several other employees from the rafting company. "What's going on?" he asked incredulously. It wasn't his birthday. That had come and gone without anyone knowing about it. They all marched in and occupied the few chairs he had as well as the floor. They tore into the pizza—a meatza loaded with everything.

"We got our place back!" Todd said with his mouth full of pizza.

"What Todd means is, the lawsuit's been dropped," Jo added. "Neil helped out. The case is closed."

"I want you back, Dan," Todd added. "I've got big plans to turn the company into a family-friendly business. With you and Jo at the helm, it's gonna be great!"

Dan sat there with a piece of half-eaten pizza on his plate. It had all come crashing down so suddenly, he didn't know what to say or think. When he stayed silent, everyone stopped eating and stared at him.

"Something wrong?" Todd asked. His eyes narrowed in

concern. "Look, I'm sorry I had to let you go, Dan. I hope you'll forgive me for doing it. I didn't have a choice. . . ."

He continued to sit in silence until his gaze focused on the bare wall where the TV once hung. The empty place where the sofa stood. He could have it all back. He could have his old life, complete with his board shorts and shades. His Jeep, which he sorely missed. The kids loving him as he manned the helm of a raft. And Jo by his side.

"I'll have to think about it, Todd."

In an instant the joy of the celebration evaporated. Within a half hour, the group began to break up. Dan felt no remorse for what he'd said. But he couldn't say yes. Not now. When Todd left, Jo still sat cross-legged on the floor, looking up at him in curiosity.

"So what's going on, Dan? I can't believe you're not jumping all over this."

"God."

Jo sucked in her breath.

"I wasn't swearing. God is doing something in me, Jo, something big. I know I should be throwing another huge party with this announcement of getting back to the river and all. But like you said, I used the river as an escape. A problem solver. If I went back to the river, I'd still be floating in the same old raft of trouble." He paused. "I–I need to make a visit home."

Jo sat still, with a face he couldn't begin to read in a million years. He thought she would be happy for him. But instead, he watched a pool of tears collect in her soft brown eyes and roll down her cheeks.

"Jo, please. It's not like I don't want to be with you and help your cousin. . ."

"Oh, Dan, it's not that. It's just. . .I've been praying, too.

Asking God what to do about my life. The mistakes I've made in the past. And if I should go back. I think you just gave me the answer."

"But you shouldn't be doing what I'm doing."

"Yeah, I should. We're more alike than you think. Just because I talk the God-talk doesn't mean I always walk the God-walk. I needed someone to take me by the spiritual hand and lead me. I knew in my heart I had to confront my brother Ross. To tell him I'm sorry and thank him for everything he's done. And make amends with my parents, too, and ask for their forgiveness."

"I need to do that." He paused. "Okay, so when do we buy our plane tickets? Bet if I ask Rob, he'll let me have the cash for it. He's got another job besides the farm and is making decent money now."

Jo stood to her feet and drew forward. His arms curled around her. Suddenly they were kissing, not in pent-up passion or for any other reason, but in thankfulness for the decision they had made.

fifteen

He could not believe his nerves. He, Dan the man, was now Dan the soul of humility. He was doing what he thought impossible in days gone by. He was going home to reconcile what was and see where God might be leading him next. He wished then that Jo had come with him, but she had her own time of reconciliation to perform. They parted ways at the airport where he caught a flight to Richmond and she to Dulles near DC. But before that, they shared a kiss and vowed to pray for each other. How Dan needed that prayer now. His hands tensed around the steering wheel of the rental car he'd picked up at the Richmond airport. He'd not let his folks know he was coming back home. Rob knew, of course. He'd loaned Dan the money to make the trip. He hoped it wouldn't be too much of a shocker on his folks, but this needed to be done.

Soon the familiar green fields he'd seen all his life began to materialize before him. It looked as if the ground had received a good soaking of rain. He hoped Pop would have a good harvest. He wanted the man to receive God's blessings in his life. And he realized then how much he'd been blessed by his father's hard work. He never lacked for anything. And yet he had taken all of the hard-earned money and spent it on frivolous things. Sure, some of the money was his. He'd worked for it. But really, they'd all worked for it by way of managing the farm they called their own.

A tear or two teased his eyes, wondering what would happen.

His hands trembled as he turned onto the road leading to the Mallory farm. In the field ahead, Rob was driving the tractor—the one Dan crushed the peanut plants with in the days leading up to his exodus from this place. He brought the car to a stop and sat watching his brother. The tractor rolled along with Rob oblivious of his arrival. He waited until Rob turned the tractor around and drove it back in his direction. The engine hissed and groaned. It then came to a stop. He saw a figure stand up. And then Rob jumped down.

"Dan! Wow, it's so good to see you, bro." Rob gave Dan the strongest hug he'd ever received.

"Do Mom and Pop know I'm coming home?" Dan asked.

"No. I kept it a surprise for them. Come on back to the house. They will be so glad to see you." Rob turned serious. "But I need to tell you something, Dan. Pop isn't well. His heart's been acting up. We just found out yesterday he may need surgery. I knew you were on your way here, so I waited to tell you in person."

Dan stopped walking. "His heart's not right?" he managed to croak out.

"Yeah. He had some tests done and the results came back. They say there's a blockage or something in a few arteries. He has to go for more tests."

"Maybe I shouldn't see him now. I don't want to cause him any more stress."

"I think you're just the right medicine for him. He's missed you a lot."

Dan wished that were true, but he couldn't help thinking what a disappointment he'd been to his parents, leaving them as he did, wasting his inheritance, not being there to help when they needed him most. With the work Rob could not do in his absence, Pop was obliged to handle it. For all he knew, Dan was to blame for his father's heart condition. His trepidation at the reunion was now magnified. He slowed his feet to a snail's pace as Rob went ahead of him to announce his presence.

Mom came running out, clad in her frilled apron, her arms extended. "Oh, my boy! My precious boy. And I don't care how old you are; you're still my boy. I'm so glad you're home."

"Hey Mom," was all he managed to croak out. His beloved, praying mom who never gave up hope, no matter where life carried him. He used to make fun of her godliness. Now he relished it. She smelled good, too, like moms usually do, of fine cooking and flowers and a hominess he couldn't begin to describe.

She took up his hand. "Come on into the house. Your father will be so glad to see you."

"I'm not so sure. I don't. . .I don't want his heart acting up because of me."

"It will be all right. Go on in and see him. He's in the den. And we're having your favorite dinner, too."

Dan couldn't help the tear that trickled down his cheek. *God, I don't deserve any of this*, he thought. He stopped short at the doorway to the den where Pop sat in his easy chair, reading the newspaper.

"Hi, Pop," he managed to say.

The paper fell into his lap. "Dan." He stood to his feet. "Son, you're back."

"It's okay. Don't hurt yourself."

"I'm fine. Especially now. Come on in. Sit here. Tell me how you are."

Dan did so, slowly. "I wish I could say that everything is fine, Pop. I did find a job but also did some dumb things. Thought I was a hotshot, really. Made some stupid decisions.

I—I spent all the money you gave me. And when I needed it most, it was all gone. But then there was the whole beginning. Leaving you all like I did. And I know I'm responsible in large part for your heart problems." The tears came fast and furious. "I've caused you all kinds of pain and stress and—"

"Son, you're home, and you're safe. That's the only thing that matters." He paused. "You look like skin and bones, son."

"Yeah, it got tough in Moab. I lost my job. Barely made ends meet. Then I got a job hauling garbage. But it was good for me, Pop. Real good."

Pop nodded. "Things like that can be, son. They really can. God works everything together for good."

Later that evening, after a lavish dinner of pot roast with all the trimmings, Dan shared with the family about his life in Moab. Everyone listened quietly. No one offered any rebuke. No "I told you so." Or anything else. They just sat there with thoughtful faces. After it all, Rob suggested they catch the new sci-fi movie out sometime. Mom said she needed to make a run to the grocery store for more food now that her boy was home.

"I met someone special, too, in Moab," Dan went on. "Her name is Jolene. Jo for short. She's a strong Christian woman, Mom and Pop. You'd love her. She talked a lot of sense into me. I owe her so much."

"Well, when do we get to meet her?" Mom asked. "But she's in Utah, isn't she?"

"Actually she went home, too. She's up north near Leesburg. Like me, she had some things to work out with family here in Virginia."

"All things work together for good," Mom said with a smile. "Even with all our plans, God is still in control of it all."

How glad Dan was for the reminder after all he'd been

through. But now his thoughts were on Jo. He missed her a great deal and wondered how things were going for her.

A few days later, he heard from Jo. His heart beat rapidly, the love surging through him as she shared her excitement over her time at home. How she'd made amends with her brother and even gotten to speak with her parents for the first time in years. She said her mother cried. She then talked about Dan to her family, along with their adventures in Moab.

"I talked about you, too," Dan said with a laugh. "And my parents want to meet you bad."

"I'll be on the bus to Richmond tomorrow, if you want."

"Booyah!" he shouted, louder than he intended. Mom ducked in the doorway, asking if everything was all right. "Jo's coming to meet you," he told her.

Mom smiled and nodded.

❧

Jo's coming! Dan's heart sang. He couldn't wait to see her—her streaming hair, bright eyes, and magnificent smile. And to remember all they had been through together. He didn't know what would have become of his life if Jo hadn't been there. If he hadn't worked for her cousin's company. And if he hadn't personally met the God who made Arches National Park, the God of rivers and red rocks, the sun, and yes, of people like Brian and others who cared. All of it made him rejoice.

When Jo arrived on the bus, she was like a vision sent from heaven. He swept her up in his arms and gave her a kiss, which she returned. He held her hand the entire time he drove back from the bus station, telling her about the reunion with his family and God's grace over it. "After it was over, all I could think about was you." He stopped at the fields on the road to the house. "This is where I come from, Jo. These are the famous peanut fields."

"Oh, it's so lush and green. No red rocks and dust. Just green everywhere. It's beautiful."

Peanut fields are beautiful? What a wild concept to him. But it showed him how different everything was now, with the right attitude in place. He parked the car. "Come see what we grow, up close and personal."

She obliged, walking the fields with him as he explained how the peanuts were grown and harvested. "So, do you think you'll live here now?" she wondered.

"I need to stay, at least for the time being. Pop's heart's not good. They need the help. Maybe when he's better. I'm hoping Brian can find me someone to sublet the house in Moab. Maybe someone from church."

Jo sucked in her breath. "You need to do what God is calling you to do."

"But Jo, I don't want you to go back to Utah and leave me here. Please, if there's any way you could stay, too?"

"Dan, even if I lived with my brother, we'd be hours away."

"Better than a thousand miles."

She shook her head. "I don't think I can."

"Then let's get married. You can be here with me."

Jo released his hand and stepped back. "What? Dan, you can't be serious."

"I have no choice but to be serious when I'm standing in a peanut field. I love you, Jo. You're the best thing that's ever happened to me. I feel alive when I'm with you. I want you to be with me, forever."

"Oh Dan." She thought for a moment. "I love you, too. It's been hard for us, I know. Lots of bumps in the road. But it's amazing to see what God has done and what He's continuing to do." She looked out over the fields. "And the way He's restoring things and making everything alive and new. But let's not rush something this important. Let's keep getting to know each other and see what God has in store for us." She thought for a moment. "I can tell Todd I need to stay here for now—he knows I came out here and had things to do. He can find others to help at the company. Maybe there's a place I can stay nearby, at least temporarily. And we'll take it from there."

Dan squeezed her hand, thankful to have God in his heart and Jo by his side. "Let's go meet the family." His gaze lifted to heaven. *Thank You, Lord. I was lost and now am found. Delivered, from stuff, from life. But most of all. . .from myself.*

A Letter To Our Readers

Dear Reader:
In order that we might better contribute to your reading enjoyment, we would appreciate your taking a few minutes to respond to the following questions. We welcome your comments and read each form and letter we receive. When completed, please return to the following:

Fiction Editor
Heartsong Presents
PO Box 719
Uhrichsville, Ohio 44683

1. Did you enjoy reading *Love's Winding Path* by Lauralee Bliss?
   ❑ Very much! I would like to see more books by this author!
   ❑ Moderately. I would have enjoyed it more if

   ____

   ____

   ____

2. Are you a member of **Heartsong Presents**? ❑ Yes ❑ No
   If no, where did you purchase this book? ______________

   ____

3. How would you rate, on a scale from 1 (poor) to 5 (superior), the cover design? ______________________

4. On a scale from 1 (poor) to 10 (superior), please rate the following elements.

____ Heroine	____ Plot
____ Hero	____ Inspirational theme
____ Setting	____ Secondary characters

5. These characters were special because? ________________

____

____

6. How has this book inspired your life? ________________

____

____

7. What settings would you like to see covered in future **Heartsong Presents** books? ________________________

____

____

8. What are some inspirational themes you would like to see treated in future books? ________________________

____

____

9. Would you be interested in reading other **Heartsong Presents** titles? ❑ Yes ❑ No

10. Please check your age range:

❑ Under 18 ❑ 18-24
❑ 25-34 ❑ 35-45
❑ 46-55 ❑ Over 55

Name ____
Occupation ___________________________________
Address ______________________________________
City, State, Zip _______________________________
E-mail _______________________________________